Awards and Praise for

THE SISTERS GRIMM SERIES:

Today Show Kids Book Club Pick
New York Times Bestseller
Book Sense Pick

★ "The twists and turns of the plot, the clever humor, and the behind-the-scenes glimpses of Everafters we think we know will appeal to many readers." —*Kliatt*, starred review

★ "Terrific, head-spinning series . . . Rich in well-set-up surprises and imaginatively tweaked characters . . ." —*Kirkus*, starred review

"Enormously entertaining, the book takes the fractured fairy-tale genre to new heights." —*Time Out New York Kids*

"Adventure, laughs, and surprises kept me eagerly turning the pages." —R. L. Stine, author of *Goosebumps*

BY MICHAEL BUCKLEY:

In the *Sisters Grimm* series:

BOOK ONE: THE FAIRY-TALE DETECTIVES

BOOK TWO: THE UNUSUAL SUSPECTS

BOOK THREE: THE PROBLEM CHILD

BOOK FOUR: ONCE UPON A CRIME

BOOK FIVE: MAGIC AND OTHER MISDEMEANORS

BOOK SIX: TALES FROM THE HOOD

BOOK SEVEN: THE EVERAFTER WAR

BOOK EIGHT: THE INSIDE STORY

BOOK NINE: THE COUNCIL OF MIRRORS

A VERY GRIMM GUIDE

In the *NERDS* series:

BOOK ONE: NATIONAL ESPIONAGE, RESCUE,
AND DEFENSE SOCIETY

BOOK TWO: M IS FOR MAMA'S BOY

BOOK THREE: CHEERLEADERS OF DOOM

THE SISTERS GRIMM

· BOOK EIGHT ·

THE INSIDE STORY

MICHAEL BUCKLEY

PICTURES BY PETER FERGUSON

AMULET BOOKS

New York

The Library of Congress has cataloged the hardcover edition of this book as follows:

Buckley, Michael.
The sisters Grimm, book 8 : the inside story / Michael Buckley ; pictures by Peter Ferguson.
p. cm.
Summary: As the fairytale detectives race through the Book of Everafter searching for their baby brother, they encounter various characters including the Editor and his army of revisers, who threaten the children with dire consequences if they continue to change the stories.
ISBN 978-0-8109-8430-1
[1. Sisters—Fiction. 2. Magic—Fiction. 3. Books and reading—Fiction. 4. Characters in literature—Fiction. 5. Mystery and detective stories.] I. Ferguson, Peter, 1968– ill. II. Title.
III. Title: The sisters Grimm, book eight.
PZ7.B882323
[Fic]—dc22
2009052207

Paperback ISBN 978-0-8109-9726-4

Text copyright © 2010 Michael Buckley
Illustrations copyright © 2010 Peter Ferguson

Printed and bound in U.S.A.
10 9 8 7 6 5 4 3 2

Amulet Books are available at special discounts when purchased in quantity for premiums and promotions as well as fundraising or educational use. Special editions can also be created to specification. For details, contact specialsales@abramsbooks.com or the address below.

THE ART OF BOOKS SINCE 1949
115 West 18th Street
New York, NY 10011
www.abramsbooks.com

For two very good editors,
Susan Van Metre and Maggie Lehrman

Acknowledgments

This book was the most difficult of the series to write, even with the considerable help of the geniuses who came long before me. First, thanks to Carlo Collodi's masterpiece *The Adventures of Pinocchio*, and also to Sir Richard F. Burton's translation of *The Arabian Nights*, L. Frank Baum's *Wonderful Wizard of Oz*, as well as Rudyard Kipling's *Jungle Book*, Washington Irving's "Legend of Sleepy Hollow," and Lewis Carroll's *Alice's Adventures in Wonderland*. *The Annotated Brothers Grimm*, edited and translated by Maria Tatar, was also essential to this writing. Unfortunately, there are tales I used whose authors have faded from our collective knowledge, but their spirits visited me and I thank them for their timeless stories.

I want to thank my editors, Susan Van Metre and Maggie Lehrman, for their incredible patience. Without their many, many, many extensions (and efforts to prevent my nervous breakdown), I would not have been able to finish. I also want to thank everyone at Abrams for their incredible support, including Michael Jacobs and Howard Reeves, the marketing and sales departments, and my publicists, Jason Wells, Mary Ann Zissimos, and Laura Mihalick. Much thanks to Chad Beckerman for his amazing vision and talent.

There is also my agent and wife, the amazing, talented, and

beautiful Alison Fargis of the Stonesong Press; my good friend Joe Deasy, who reads and rereads these books; my family; my good friend Josh Drisko, who keeps me laughing at myself; and Mary Brown, Jessie Harper, and Erica Alicea at Starbucks #11807 on Smith Street in Brooklyn.

But above all, thanks to my son, Finn, who inspires a million stories with every smile.

THE SISTERS GRIMM

BOOK EIGHT

THE INSIDE STORY

THE FIRST EXPLOSION *sent Sabrina flailing backward to the floor of the ancient tomb. Her head slammed against the stone and her sneakers were blasted off her feet. Before she could stand up, there was a second explosion. The noise rattled her eardrums and a blast of wind scorched her face, neck, and hands. But the third explosion was the one that really frightened her. It split columns in two and churned the ground like a pot of boiling water. Fissures formed, allowing skin-searing steam to escape from deep below. Along with it came an unearthly concoction of lights and sounds and colors. It wasn't a mist or a fog—it was alive, made from something old and angry. It spun into a whirlwind and surrounded Sabrina's ragtag crowd of would-be heroes.*

"This is not good!" Daphne shouted over the din. "We have to stop it."

"Be my guest!" Sabrina cried. "If you haven't noticed, I don't have any magical powers. I'm not an Everafter. I'm just a girl from New York City."

Sabrina searched her mind for an idea, a notion, a plan—but there was nothing. Why was she drawing a blank? This wasn't her first end-of-the-world scenario. She had always managed to find a solution before. Where were all her brilliant ideas when she needed them?

There was a fourth and final explosion, and something inside the odd swirling gases began to pulsate. A loud, pounding rhythm, not unlike a heartbeat, filled Sabrina's ears. The light and sound and color formed into a single being with eyes like a bottomless pit and a smile that chilled her bones.

It was too late. He had his freedom and Sabrina could feel the world trembling.

1

THREE DAYS EARLIER
(OR HALF AN HOUR . . . IT'S ALL IN HOW YOU LOOK AT IT)

aphne, I don't think we're in Ferryport Landing anymore," Sabrina Grimm said. Without waiting for an answer, she grabbed her sister's hand and ran back to the wooden farmhouse. Once inside, she slammed the door shut and leaned against it. The farmhouse was small and rustic, with dirt floors and shabby furniture—three chairs, a rickety table, two tiny beds, an iron stove, and a frayed rug. What little light managed to slip through the windows was overwhelmed by shadows, and there was a thick cloud of poverty hanging over everything. To call it a house would have been generous. It was more like a shack.

"Daphne?"

"I'm OK," her sister's voice called back. "They're singing for us."

Sabrina clambered up atop one of the beds, where Daphne stood. Her little sister was wearing a yellow dress and pushing a pair of creaky shutters open in order to peer out into the sunshine. She smiled brightly, her eyes filled with curiosity. Sabrina envied Daphne's attitude. Her sister was much better at adapting to the twists and turns to which the two sisters were often subjected. She seemed to lack suspicion or worry, but Sabrina had a never-ending supply. Unfortunately, Daphne also lacked the necessary wariness their lives often required.

"Get away from the window," Sabrina scolded.

Daphne giggled and then bit down on the palm of her hand. It was a quirky habit that came out when she was very excited or very happy. From the look of the bite mark she now had, it appeared she was both. "We're here. We're actually here!"

"Where's here?" Sabrina asked as she climbed down from the bed and slowly opened the front door again. A breeze swept into the shack, swirling a cyclone of dust on the floor. Standing on the stoop outside was a very short, very chubby old woman who resembled a baked potato stuffed in a white dress. Accompanying her was a trio of equally tiny men. Each had the face of a cherub, except for their bushy white beards and untamed eyebrows. None was taller than three feet, and all were dressed in matching blue suits and pie-tin–shaped hats. Behind them, Sabrina could see a town square lined with little round houses the same color as the tiny people's suits and hats. The square had a road leading away from it paved with yellow bricks. A Yellow Brick Road.

"Welcome—"

Sabrina slammed the door in their faces. "We're in Oz!"

"I know! It's awesome."

"No, Daphne, it's not awesome. All the people from Oz are crazy!"

"I know how much people from Oz annoy you, but think about it. We're actually in the Land of Oz, or I guess, we're technically in the story of Oz. I didn't believe it was possible when Mirror told us about the Book of Everafter, but he was telling the truth. We're inside a book of fairy tales!"

Sabrina bristled at the mention of Mirror's name, and a wave of sadness swept over her. She felt her throat tighten as she fought back tears. She never wanted to hear that man's name again.

"I wonder when Dorothy will show up," Daphne continued, still grinning.

"Try to focus," Sabrina insisted. "The reason we're in this

story is to find Mirror and save our baby brother from whatever wicked plan Mirror has cooking in his stupid bald head. We don't have time for some idiot from Kansas."

Daphne frowned. "OK, so what's the plan?"

Sabrina sat down on one of the creaky beds and stared at the empty wall. "I don't know."

"I'm sorry," Daphne said, "but did the great Sabrina Grimm just say she didn't know what to do?"

Sabrina understood her sister was teasing, but she couldn't bring herself to smile. The few options they had felt murky and confusing. Should they chase Mirror in hopes of rescuing the baby, or stay put and hope the rest of their family would show up to help? She and Daphne knew next to nothing about the Book of Everafter. How did it work? What were the rules of the Book? Could they be injured—or worse, killed? The Grimm sisters had a hard enough time staying alive in the real world. Could they survive in a magic book? And then there were the others to consider: Pinocchio, who had betrayed them, and Puck. Both had stepped into the Book alongside them, but where were they now? Dead? Injured? Lost? Should she and her sister wait for them to show up, or start searching for them, too? There were too many questions and too much still unknown to answer them. What if Sabrina made the wrong choice?

Two years ago, Sabrina and Daphne had a simple, happy life on the Upper East Side of Manhattan, in New York City, when their parents disappeared. Overnight, Sabrina was enrolled in a crash course on taking care of her little sister, being tough, and thinking on her feet in order to survive the foster care system. The sisters were bounced from one cruel and crazy family to the next, finally landing in the home of an eccentric old woman who turned out to be the grandmother they never knew they had.

Granny Relda, as they called her, lived in a tiny town on the Hudson River called Ferryport Landing. There was no point looking it up on a map, as it wasn't on most—and for good reason. Most of the town's inhabitants were the real-life people so many fairy tales were based upon. Witches ran the local diner. Ogres delivered the mail. The Queen of Hearts was the town's mayor. With a population so strange and magical, it was best if everyone kept a low profile.

Granny Relda filled the girls in on their equally fascinating family history. She was a detective, a fairy-tale detective to be exact, just like all the Grimms before her. Their ancestors, the Brothers Grimm, had been detectives too, investigating the strange and magical cases they encountered. If the world thought their book was a collection of bedtime stories, it was probably for the best, because the truth would keep everyone up at night.

The girls had lived with Granny Relda for almost a year, and in that time she trained them to take over the family business. It was dangerous work. The girls learned that sometimes the good guys were villains and sometimes the bad guys were their greatest allies. Sabrina never really let her guard down and continued to call the shots for her sister and herself. Inevitably, she butted heads with her grandmother and nearly everyone else they met. When her mother and father were returned to her, she saw it as an opportunity to go back to being a normal kid. She should have known better. As Grimms, they could never be sure what danger might appear around the next corner.

"Well, we can't sit here all day, I guess. We should go outside and see if Mirror and Sammy are in this story," Daphne said.

"Sammy?" Sabrina asked.

"We can't call the baby 'what's-his-name,'" Daphne said. "You don't like the name Sammy?"

Sabrina shrugged. "Whatever. The real problem is that this could be dangerous, Daphne. Some of the stories in this book aren't exactly kid friendly. A lot of them are pretty . . . well, twisted. What if we step through one of these doors and walk into Bluebeard's house or onto the plank on Long John Silver's boat?"

"We'll kick butt and take names like we always do," the little girl said, stepping into the karate stance she had learned in a self-defense class.

Sabrina wished she could muster the same confidence. "I'm just saying we need to be careful. One look around and you can see that something is off. The colors are weird. Everything is too bright and cheery, and there are too many things with the same color. There are flowers in the square the same color blue as the houses. The Munchkins outside look strange too. Like the details aren't all there."

"So the colors are off. I don't think we have anything to fear from the color blue," Daphne said.

"What I'm saying is this book has its own rules. Like the dress you're wearing: You didn't have that on when we stepped into the Book."

Daphne looked down at the yellow dress she wore, and then back to her sister. "So the Book changed my clothes. Big deal."

"If it can do that, what else can it do?"

"It didn't change you at all."

Sabrina was still wearing her jeans, sneakers, and sweater. She had no explanation.

Daphne continued. "Unfortunately, big sister, the only way to learn the rules is to get started." She pointed out the window to a sea of Munchkins that had circled the house.

Sabrina groaned. "Fine! But stay close. And just so you know, I have no problem serving up a plate of knuckle sandwiches to these weirdoes if they get in the way—whether they're real or not!"

Daphne opened the door and a crowd of Munchkins gaped in wonder, letting out a collective "*Oooohhhhhhhh!*" The lumpy old woman in white hobbled forward. She cleared her throat and bowed as low as her old bones would allow. "You are welcome, most noble Sorceress, to the land of the Munchkins. We are so grateful to you for having killed the Wicked Witch of the East, and for setting our people free from bondage."

"No problem," Sabrina said, rolling her eyes at Daphne. "So, we're looking for a man carrying a small boy. Has anyone seen them?"

The Munchkins seemed startled by her response, as if they were waiting for a different reply.

"Wait a minute! We killed who?" Daphne shouted as she pushed through the crowd. Sabrina followed, and the girls rounded the side of the little farmhouse. Sticking out from beneath the house was a pair of legs wearing bright silver shoes.

"Call 911!" Daphne cried as she knelt beside the feet.

"There is nothing to be done," the squat woman in white said in an irritating singsong voice. "She was the Wicked Witch of the East. She held all the Munchkins in bondage for many years, making them slave for her night and day. Now they are all set free and are grateful for the favor."

Daphne ignored her and shouted at the feet. "Don't worry, lady! We'll get you out of there."

One of the tiny men stepped forward. "That's not the line."

Sabrina and Daphne eyed one another, confused. "Huh?"

The woman in white looked around her and then leaned in close and whispered in a voice no louder than a mouse. "That's not what you say. You're supposed to ask me if I'm a Munchkin. That's what happens next."

Sabrina scowled and clenched her fists. "What is she talking about? Every person from this nutty place is—"

Daphne turned to the little woman. "OK, we'll say what you want us to say. Are you a Munchkin?"

The woman sighed in great relief and smoothed some wrinkles out of her dress. "No, but I am their friend. When they saw the Wicked Witch of the East was dead, the Munchkins sent a swift messenger to me, and I came at once. I am the Witch of the North."

"I thought Glinda was the Witch of the North," Sabrina said.

Daphne shook her head. "That's the movie. Glinda's the Witch of the South. Haven't you read this story?"

"I skimmed it."

Another of the little men chimed in. "No, you're supposed to say 'Oh gracious! Are you a real witch?'"

Sabrina fumed and stomped her foot. "Just let me punch one of them out. It will be a lesson for the others."

"Silence your animal, Dorothy!" another Munchkin demanded. "This is not what happened."

"Dorothy?" Sabrina said.

"My name's not—wait! They think I'm Dorothy," Daphne said as a happy smile spread across her face. "The Book must have turned us into characters."

"Then who am I?" Sabrina said as she studied her clothing.

Daphne snickered. "Probably Toto."

Sabrina started to smile, but it quickly turned to a frown. She reached under her shirt and found a small leather collar fastened around her neck. A silver tag engraved with the name "Toto" was attached. She pulled it off and angrily threw it to the ground. "Of course! *I* have to be the dog."

Daphne laughed so hard she snorted.

"Yes, it's hilarious," Sabrina steamed. "Don't be surprised if I bite your leg."

Daphne got herself under control. "Well, this is interesting. If the Book is turning us into the characters, maybe that's everyone's problem. We're supposed to follow the story. Am I right?"

The crowd eyed them quietly as if afraid to answer. Finally, one of the little old men nodded subtly and whispered, "Please, we beg you. Just say the line."

Sabrina threw up her hands in frustration and turned to her sister. "I feel like I'm trapped in a second-grade play. They're going to have to spoon-feed us every line of dialogue unless you've got this story memorized from beginning to end."

Daphne ignored her and recited the line the Munchkin had given to her. "'Oh gracious! Are you a real witch?'"

"Yes indeed," the woman in white said. "But I am a good witch, and the people love me. I am not as powerful as the Wicked Witch was who ruled here, or I should have set the people free myself."

Sabrina groaned. "Enough! We're not here to be part of your story. We're looking for a man who is traveling with a toddler—a little boy. Have you seen them or not?"

The Munchkins leaped back in fright.

"He's short and balding and wearing a black suit," Daphne added.

A rosy-cheeked man in the back of the crowd made his way to the front. "I have seen him."

The rest of the Munchkins broke into excited complaints, begging their friend to be quiet and not change the story. He spat on the ground and refused. "It's best to just get them out of here as soon as possible," he said. "They're just like the last fellow. He wouldn't follow the story either."

"Mirror was here? Are you sure?"

"Didn't ask his name, young lady, but there was a man this way not long ago," the Munchkin said. "He took off down the Yellow Brick Road in search of the magic door."

"Magic door?"

"It pops up at the end of the story. Never seen it myself, but I've heard rumors it can take you out of this story and into the next."

Sabrina turned to her sister. "Then we have to stop him. If he gets to the door, who knows where he'll end up next."

"How do we find this door?" Daphne said.

The nervous crowd looked at one another. After several moments of talking amongst themselves, the woman in white stepped close.

"You have to clean those ears of yours. The man said it pops up at the end of the story. The best way to find it is to just do everything that happened the first time, like it was when the real Dorothy did it. Go down the Yellow Brick Road, find your companions, enter the Emerald City, and meet the great and terrible Wizard of Oz. He'll send you to kill the Wicked Witch of the West. Once that's done, the door should appear."

"That will take forever," Sabrina complained.

"Isn't there another way?" Daphne asked the Witch.

The old woman shook her head violently. "I've said too much already. I'll anger the Editor."

"The Editor?" Daphne asked.

Everyone shushed her at once. "Don't say his name! You'll call attention to us!"

Sabrina rolled her eyes. "C'mon. We're wasting time with these nutcases. Let's go."

Daphne nodded. "Well, nice to meet you all. Sorry to kill that witch and just run off, but we're really in a hurry."

With that, the girls turned and headed toward the square and the winding Yellow Brick Road beyond. But it wasn't long before they were stopped in their tracks by angry shouts.

When they spun around, the girls found a stout Munchkin with a red face and a long beard, which he repeatedly tripped over as he rushed in their direction. When he finally reached them, he bent over to catch his breath and handed Daphne the silver slippers that were previously on the Witch's feet.

"You forgot these," he gasped. "They're a big part of this story, you know."

"Thanks," Daphne said sheepishly.

"Oh, and do yourself a favor—stay inside the margins," he said.

"The margins?"

"Yes, you know, stay in the story. Don't wander around in parts that weren't written down."

"Why?" Sabrina said.

"Because . . . it's dangerous!" the little man shouted. "Do you need an explanation for everything? Stay inside the story and you'll be safe."

Before Daphne could thank him for his advice, he turned and stomped back to the village, muttering insults.

"He's so pleasant," Sabrina said.

"C'mon, Toto," Daphne said with a wink. "We've got a bad guy to catch and a little brother to rescue. Be a good dog and I'll scratch your belly later."

"Keep it up and I swear I'll dig a hole and bury you in it," Sabrina grumbled.

Daphne grinned. "Bad dog. I might have to swat you with a rolled-up newspaper."

• • •

The countryside of Oz was both spectacular and strange. Ancient trees lined the roads, each with burly knots and cracks that gave them the appearance of faces. Wild birds of unusual colors flew overhead. One bird's plumage had a black-and-white checkered pattern. It landed on the path and eyed them curiously, as if they were the peculiar ones. Each bend in the road brought a new strange animal or freckling of unfamiliar flowers. Sabrina enjoyed the light breeze—it was the cleanest she had ever smelled. It had a calm, warm flavor like fresh oatmeal cookies and vanilla, and it swept across fields lush with wild grasses.

The scenery helped pass the time, though its strange colors and somewhat unreal appearance started to give Sabrina a headache. They walked on for the better part of a day, keeping careful eyes on the Yellow Brick Road for signs that Mirror had passed ahead of them. Their former friend left nothing obvious, which made Sabrina quietly fret that he had taken their little brother off the path to hide inside the ancient woods that lined the road. She didn't know much about Oz, but she sensed it was big. Mirror and the baby could be anywhere.

By dusk, their first sign of intelligent life came into view—a family of Munchkins living in one of the now-familiar circular houses. The man of the house was a short, shiny-faced fellow named Boq. He invited them to dinner. Though the two girls were famished, they declined. Daphne tried to explain their need to find Mirror, but like the others they had met, he was intent on keeping to the story. After much arguing, he informed the girls that Dorothy and Toto were supposed to eat and stay the night. When they refused, again, he chased them down the road for a mile and a half, begging them to return. Eventually, he gave up and walked back the way he had come with a defeated and worried expression.

"They're all freaked out about this Editor dude," Daphne said.

Sabrina didn't recall a character named the Editor in any of L. Frank Baum's famous accounts of the Land of Oz, but then again, she barely knew the first book, and there were thirteen more she had just flipped through.

• • •

Soon the setting sun turned the sky into a canvas of crimsons, rusts, and tangerines. The girls found a clear space beneath a fruit tree. Ravenous, they shook at its limbs and collected the plump and curious fruits that fell. There were apples and oranges, but also many bizarre fruits Sabrina had never seen. Daphne happily munched on them all, but Sabrina turned her nose up at the most strange.

"I wasn't sure we could eat these," Daphne said between bites. "I thought maybe they weren't real."

"It's funny what's real and what's not. These taste just like fruit from Granny's kitchen. But look around. It's like we're walking through a painting or the illustrations in a book."

"Like someone else's memory," Daphne said.

Sabrina agreed. That was exactly the best way to explain how everything looked. It was like strolling around in someone's distant memory. Perhaps that's why everything felt strange and a little incomplete.

The girls ate until their bellies were full. Then they lay down under the tree and looked up at the unfamiliar constellations in Oz's sky, another reminder of their strange environment.

"I'm worried about Puck," Daphne said.

Sabrina grunted, not wanting her sister to suspect her concern about the boy fairy.

"I keep having this terrible thought," Daphne continued. "If the Book has turned me into Dorothy and you're Toto, what if that dead witch back in Munchkinland was him?"

"That wasn't him. We would have recognized his stink. Even a dead witch's corpse smells better than Puck. If we're lucky, that was Pinocchio sticking out from under that house."

Daphne hissed. "I can't believe he was working with the Master. I mean, Mirror. Whoever."

"It makes me wonder who I can trust," Sabrina whispered. She felt her sister's hand slide into her own. It helped unravel the knot of worry in Sabrina's belly a little.

"You can trust me," Daphne said. "And you can trust Sammy."

Sabrina's heart sank a little. Whenever she thought about the little boy and Mirror's cruel plans, she felt ill. "I doubt he has a name," she replied. "Mirror doesn't see him as a person. He's just a body. To him, our little brother is nothing more than a box for his soul. Don't forget, he let Red Riding Hood babysit when she was at her craziest."

"Well, I'm naming him. Do you think Mom and Dad will mind?"

Sabrina chuckled. "Probably. I think that's one of the perks of having kids. You get to name them."

Daphne sighed. "You're probably right. Still, he needs a name. Mom and Dad can rename him when we get him home."

"Fine, but I vote against Sammy Grimm," Sabrina said. "You remember Sammy from the orphanage?"

Sammy Cartwright was a bed-wetter, but not, unfortunately, when he was in his own bed. Sabrina could still remember leaping into her cot only to find herself swimming in damp sheets.

Daphne cringed. "How could I forget Soggy Sammy? I'll get to work on a better name."

A moment later, she was sleeping deeply, the hum of her snoring drifting into the tree branches above. Sabrina closed her eyes and tried to imagine her brother. He would have red hair, like her grandmother Relda, and round cheeks, like her father and Daphne. But he would also have her mother's eyes; eyes like Sabrina had too. Sadly, it was impossible to imagine his innocent little face without Mirror holding him in his arms. She had only met the boy once, and for only a brief moment, but losing him felt like losing a limb.

But Mirror had stolen more than her baby brother. His betrayal had robbed her of her best friend, too. With monsters, madmen, and mermaids running around the town, there had been one constant—one confidant—for Sabrina: Mirror. Sabrina had turned to him more times than she could count. He had always been happy to see her and had been quick with good advice. He was, she thought, her one true friend, but it had all been a lie. With every smile and kind word, he had been plotting and scheming against her and her family—every betrayal and attack the Grimms faced could be traced back to Mirror.

What hurt more was that Sabrina hadn't seen it coming. She prided herself on her instincts. She could smell a rotten egg long before anyone else, but she had been wrong about Mirror. Now every decision she had made in the last two years was in doubt. All of the responsibility she had—taking care of Daphne, keeping them safe, and now saving her brother—it was all too much. She was just a kid! How could she stop Mirror's plan? He was so powerful and clever.

She knew she needed a plan, but thinking about it made her nauseated. Her heart beat too rapidly and she felt as if she couldn't get enough air into her lungs. How could she lead when nearly every choice she had made in recent history had been a horrible mistake?

• • •

The morning arrived sooner than expected. Sleeping on the ground had made the girls achy and stiff, but they knew there was no time to complain. They collected more of the weird fruit and shoved as much as they could into their pockets. Daphne found a stream and the girls drank greedily and washed their faces and hands. Then they were off, once more, down the Yellow Brick Road.

"We've been here a whole day," Sabrina said as she eyed the rising sun. "Everyone out there in the real world is going to freak out. They have no idea where we are. It could take weeks to search every room in the Hall of Wonders before they find the Book of Everafter. And then what if they don't figure out how to get into the stories?"

"You forget we come from a very smart family," Daphne said. "Granny Relda will figure it out in no time, and Mom and Dad are like geniuses. I wouldn't be surprised if we ran into them on the way to the Emerald City."

Sabrina shook her head. "I think smarts don't count for much in this book—what they need is a whole lot of luck. It seems pretty random. When you step into the Book, you could literally end up anywhere. That might explain where Puck and Pinocchio are—they may have been dropped into a completely different story. The same thing could happen to our family. I hate to say it, but I think it would be best if they just stayed where they are. The last thing we need is our whole family as lost as we are."

"I wouldn't count on that," Daphne said. "Our family isn't known for its patience."

They walked for hours until finally coming across a farm bordered by a picket fence. Not far from the road, mounted on a large pole, was a scarecrow. He had a friendly face painted on an old burlap sack, and he wore a goofy blue hat like so many of the Munchkins had been wearing. A crow was perched on his head, pecking at his face. Sabrina recognized the scarecrow at once. She knew his real-life alter ego. The Scarecrow was Ferryport Landing's librarian, and he was also a walking disaster. His klutzy behavior and accident-prone nature drove Sabrina crazy. She expected no different from his storybook twin.

He sprang to life and shooed the pesky bird away, then smiled and waved at the girls.

"Good day," he said as he lifted his head to speak to them.

"Just ignore him," Sabrina said as she tried to usher her sister along.

Daphne stopped. "We can't ignore him. We need to get him down. You heard the Munchkins. We're supposed to stick to the story. He's supposed to come with us."

Sabrina shook her head. "Absolutely not! We're not making a lot of progress as it is, and this idiot will slow us to a crawl. Besides, you know how he is."

The Scarecrow looked confused by their conversation. "You're supposed to say—"

"Yeah, we know what we're supposed to say," Sabrina said.

The Scarecrow's painted eyes grew wide with astonishment. "Would you help me down?" he asked shyly.

Daphne gave Sabrina a pleading look, but she shook her head. The little girl frowned and stepped closer to the fence. "I'm sorry, Mr. Scarecrow, but we can't. We're trying to rescue our brother and you, well, how can I put this—"

"What?"

"You're a royal pain in the behind," Sabrina interrupted.

"Your dog is quite noisy," the Scarecrow said.

"Toto says you're a pain in the behind," Daphne said.

"You dirty little fleabag!" The Scarecrow squirmed and struggled, but could not free himself from his post.

Sabrina took her sister by the hand and pulled her down the road. "You're on your own, Scarecrow. Good luck!"

"Wait!" he cried. "I didn't mean it."

"See you later," Sabrina said.

"You need me for the rest of the story," he cried, but Sabrina was determined to put as much distance between them and the insufferable stuffed man as she could. His desperate cries lingered for another ten minutes, and then he was silent.

"We should have helped him," Daphne grumbled.

"Daphne, he's not real. This whole world and everyone in it is just magic. A spell."

"Real or not, we weren't very nice to him." Her little sister was fuming. She crossed her arms in disgust and marched along in silence.

They moved away from the farmland and into a forest landscape. It wasn't long before they heard a loud groan from the trees on the side of the road.

"Did you hear that?" Daphne asked, peering through the dense trees for the source of the pained cry.

Sabrina sighed. She knew the story well enough to know who it was. "It's the Tin Man. I'm sure of it."

Daphne put her palm into her mouth and bit down. "The Tin Man is my favorite."

Sabrina shook her head. "Don't even think about it. If we left the Scarecrow, we can leave this guy too."

"We have to rescue him," the little girl cried, and then raced into the woods.

"Daphne, no!" Sabrina chased after her and soon the two girls stumbled upon a cabin in the woods. Standing nearby was the Tin Man, stiff and rusting beneath a half-chopped tree with his ax in hand. He mumbled something unintelligible, but Daphne didn't stop to try to listen. She raced into the cabin and reappeared with an oilcan in her hand. In a flash, she was squeezing black grease into the metal man's joints, and soon he was moving about freely, if not a bit awkwardly. Daphne finished her good deed with a healthy squeeze into his jaw sockets.

"I might have stood there always if you had not come along," the Tin Man said. "So you have saved my life—wait . . . someone's missing. Where's the Scarecrow?"

The girls shared a knowing look.

"Back on that pole, I suspect," Daphne said.

"You left him?" the Tin Man cried.

"We can't go through this again," Sabrina groaned. "Let's go."

"Not before I get an autograph. Do you happen to have a pen?" Daphne said to the strange man. Sabrina snatched her sister by the hand and started back to the road.

The Tin Man followed behind them. "Uh, how did you come to be here?" he sputtered.

"We're going to see the Wizard so we can kill the Wicked Witch," Daphne said.

The Tin Man stopped in his tracks. "That's not what you're supposed to say."

"We're doing things a little differently this time," Sabrina said.

"Come on, Tin Man. Come with us," Daphne pleaded.

The Tin Man reeled back on his heels. "Uh, you know, I don't really feel comfortable with that. You're not following the rules."

"Well, don't let us keep you," Sabrina called over her shoulder. She didn't bother to hide her relief.

A moment later, Sabrina noticed Daphne's arms were crossed in a huff again.

"He would slow us down," Sabrina said, though in truth she was relieved she wasn't going to have to hang out with a talking garbage can.

Daphne scowled and continued marching quietly.

As they walked, the forest swallowed the road more and more, and soon the girls found themselves beneath a canopy of limbs and leaves blocking out the sun, and a surreal sort of déjà vu took over. Sabrina knew what was about to happen from seeing the movie—one of the few fairy-tale movies her father had allowed her to see. If she remembered correctly, they were about to meet the Cowardly Lion. He would spring from the brush at any moment.

"The lion is coming," Sabrina said as she peered around.

Daphne nodded. "If he jumps out and scares me, I might wet myself. I wish we could get some kind of warning."

No sooner had she finished speaking than the monstrous beast hurled himself into the center of the road. The lion was much bigger than Sabrina had expected. His body was all muscle, and his paws were as big as tennis rackets. His enormous golden mane looked as if it could swallow a man whole, and his claws gleamed like beautiful daggers. He looked as if he were about to swat someone, but when he couldn't find his target he crouched down on his haunches. His ferocious face turned to befuddlement.

"Did you have an accident?" Sabrina asked her sister.

The little girl shook her head. "No, but it was close."

The lion furrowed his brow and let out a roar that blew the girls' hair back.

"That's not helping," Daphne continued.

Of all the parts of the wacky tale of Oz, the meeting of the Cowardly Lion was one Sabrina remembered well. "I think you have to hit him in the face. That's what happens."

Daphne shook her head. "I can't hit a lion in the face."

The lion roared loudly, then leaned over and whispered, "You have to. It's in the story."

Daphne looked perplexed. "I can't do it. It's mean."

"Fine. I have to do everything," Sabrina said as she strolled over to the lion. She pulled back and punched him square in the nose. Perhaps it was the angle of the punch, but the lion went down like a sack of potatoes and lay unconscious on the ground.

"Did you have to hit him so hard?" Daphne said, leaning over the pummeled creature.

"I barely tapped him!" Sabrina complained as she stepped over him.

"Well, we can't just leave him here in the middle of the road," Daphne said.

"You want to carry him?" Sabrina said. "He probably weighs a couple hundred pounds at least."

Daphne looked down at the hulking beast and sighed. A moment later, she stepped over the lion as well and the girls continued down the Yellow Brick Road.

"Everyone seems pretty dead set on us sticking to the story," Daphne said. "They look like they might have a breakdown when we don't."

Sabrina shrugged. "People hate change. Remember how panicked Uncle Jake was when the Butcher, the Baker, and the Candlestick Maker changed the jelly in their doughnuts from raspberry to blueberry?" Sabrina picked up the pace. "C'mon. We'll be old ladies by the time we get to the Wizard's castle."

They hadn't traveled more than a few steps when they came to a deep sinkhole in the road, nearly twenty feet across. Worse, it seemed to go on for miles in both directions. There was no way around it, and a quick glance over the edge showed it was nearly impossible to climb down.

"This is one big pothole," Daphne muttered.

"You would think that a city made out of valuable emeralds would mean you could find a little money to fix the roads," Sabrina said. "You've read this story. What did Dorothy do to get across?"

"She used us," a voice said from behind them. The girls spun around and found the Scarecrow, the Tin Man, and the Cowardly Lion approaching. They all looked very angry.

"Hey, you heard what I said!" Sabrina said. "You knew I wasn't barking."

"Of course we can hear you," the Tin Man said. "But we all have a part to play, and your part is the dog. You two are causing mayhem. You can't abandon major characters by the side of the road."

"Or in the middle of it," the Cowardly Lion growled.

"Believe it or not, we're integral parts of this tale," the Scarecrow said, as if his pride had been bruised as deeply as the lion's nose.

"You can't get through the story without our help," the Tin Man said. "And if you keep making changes, you're going to make the Editor angry."

"OK, let's hit the Rewind button here," Sabrina said. "Who is the Editor?"

"Hush!" the trio cried in a panic.

"What are you so afraid of?" Daphne asked.

The Cowardly Lion dipped his voice to a whisper. "He oversees the Book. He insists we stick to the tale. If we make changes, he will revise us. Please, just take us with you."

Daphne turned to Sabrina. "Maybe they're right. Maybe we need them."

Sabrina sighed. "Fine! But don't get in the way, and do us all a favor—stop being so persnickety about every little detail."

"He's not going to like this," the Tin Man mumbled, but still refused to explain more about the mysterious Editor. "Lion, put Dorothy and Toto on your back and jump across this ditch. When they're safe, come back and get the rest of us."

A moment later, the enormous jungle cat had jumped to the other side of the ditch and was on his way back for the others.

It was only the first in a long string of obstacles. Soon the group came across another ravine, only this one was guarded by creatures with the bodies of bears and the heads of tigers. Their claws were long and horrible, and they looked as if they could slice through a man with a flick of their wrist. The beasts followed them onto the log they used to cross the ravine, and they were preparing to pounce when the travelers shoved the downed tree over the edge, sending the monsters to their deaths.

Their next headache came in the form of a raging river. With so many people in the entourage, it took twice as long to cross as it should have. Worse, the Scarecrow insisted that he needed to strand himself on a pole in the center because that was the way it happened in real life. No matter how ridiculous and easily avoided the problems were, the three Oz characters felt compelled to follow the way things had gone the first time. Sabrina was frustrated and fuming. She knew the Scarecrow was hoping for a brain, but she was starting to think the Cowardly Lion and Tin Man might need one too. Even Daphne was irritated, and she never got angry.

But it was the poppy field that sent Sabrina's patience over the edge. She remembered the vast field from the movie and knew anyone who stepped into it would fall asleep and eventually die.

"This is insane!" Sabrina cried. "The Yellow Brick Road is the only way to the biggest city in Oz, but it's riddled with giant holes, vicious animals, a river without a bridge, and now these stupid deadly flowers. Where is the sanitation department to clean this up? You can't have these kinds of dangers on a major road!"

"Taxi service would also be a plus," Daphne added.

The Oz characters looked just as exhausted. "You and Dorothy ride on the Cowardly Lion's back for as far as he can go," the Scarecrow explained. "Then the Tin Man and I come along and rescue you. Then we meet the Queen of the Field Mice, who—"

"Queen of the Field Mice?" Sabrina said. "There's no Queen of the Field Mice!"

"It's in the book," Daphne explained.

"Well, you can just forget it!" Sabrina shouted. "If I haven't made it clear already, we aren't here to see the countryside and meet rodent royalty. We're trying to rescue our brother from a lunatic bent on stealing his body. All of this is taking too much time."

The Tin Man gasped. "But the Editor will—"

"If you tell me about your stupid Editor one more time, I'm going to melt you down and make you into hubcaps," Sabrina threatened. "We're done with you and this stupid story." Sabrina stormed off to a tree and sat down. Daphne followed and stood over her.

"So what do you want to do?" Daphne said.

Sabrina looked out over the sea of poppies and searched for an idea, any idea, but she was lost. She was satisfied after having had a good scream, but now that it was over she felt like she was stumbling through a maze that had no exit.

"This is madness. I'm sick of these idiots. I'm sick of this story and I'm sick of walking. My feet feel like they might fall off."

"Mine too," Daphne said. She sat down and took off the

witch's silver slippers. She rubbed her tired toes for a moment and then let out a scream that startled Sabrina.

"Um, duh," Daphne said as she picked up the slippers and shook them. "We could use these magic slippers! I don't know why I didn't think of it before."

Daphne slipped the shoes back on and scampered to her feet, pulling Sabrina up as well.

"I guess I thought they weren't real 'cause we're in a book," Daphne continued. "But this is no ordinary book. The fruit is real and so was the stream. Even the air we're breathing is real. If all that's real, couldn't the shoes be real too?"

Sabrina saw her sister's point. "If Dorothy's slippers work like they do in the real world, we can use them to teleport to the end of the story. We can skip all the dumb stuff and get right to the door. We could be waiting for Mirror when he and the baby arrive."

"Absolutely not!" the Scarecrow exclaimed as he stumbled over to join them.

"That is not what happens!" the Cowardly Lion cried. He was practically sobbing.

"Why do you care?" Daphne said. "We're only skipping some stuff that doesn't matter."

"Doesn't matter?" the Tin Man said. "It all matters!"

Sabrina brushed herself off and grasped her sister's arm. She looked at the others square in the eyes. "What matters is that our brother gets rescued. This train is leaving the station. Are you on or off?"

"But—" the Scarecrow cried.

Before the trio from Oz could continue their argument, a strange pink creature scurried out of the poppies. It was the size and shape of a watermelon, with long skinny arms and legs that couldn't keep its fat little body from dragging across the ground. It didn't have eyes or a nose, or at least any that Sabrina could see, but it had a big wide mouth filled with hungry teeth and a tongue that licked the air. Sabrina had never seen anything like it. She made a mental note to stop skimming the books in the family library and actually read them from cover to cover.

"Revisers!" the Scarecrow shouted.

Sabrina turned and saw the Tin Man's face. His steely expression turned to fear. "I told you not to mess with the Editor."

"Get us out of here, now!" the Cowardly Lion shouted as the pink monster scurried toward them. The three characters joined hands and clung to the girls.

Daphne clicked her heels together and repeated three times, "There's no place like the magic door."

Suddenly there was a sound like a balloon inflating almost

to bursting and the world twisted into a knot right in front of Sabrina's eyes. There was a snap and then several violent shakes. Sabrina remembered using the magic slippers out in the real world, but there had never been so much turbulence before. She found herself swirling around and around, out of control, until she staggered dizzily and the room came into focus.

She and the others were in a circular room draped in green curtains and decorated with dazzling emeralds. A throne sat high on a pedestal across from them and a bright light hovered at the top of the ceiling.

"This isn't the end of the story," Sabrina said, peering around for the door.

"This is the Wizard's castle," the Cowardly Lion said. Sabrina thought he looked as afraid of the castle as he had of the twisted pink creature they had just encountered. "The shoes did not work because the door does not exist yet. This tale is not over."

Suddenly a roaring green flame erupted in the center of the throne. Inside the flame was an enormous hovering head. It was bald with sharp features and little eyes.

"I am Oz, the Great and Terrible," the head bellowed as thunder boomed. "Who are you and why do you seek me?"

The Tin Man, the Scarecrow, and the Cowardly Lion fell over themselves in fear.

Sabrina, however, was not intimidated. She may have only skimmed the story, but everyone knew that the head was a mechanical illusion created by Oscar Diggs, also known as the Wizard, or simply, Oz. Oz had no real magical powers, but his sophisticated machines created a convincing illusion for the people of the Emerald City. He had taken over the town and ruled it with fear, but his big green floating head couldn't hurt Sabrina or her sister.

Sabrina stepped forward. "We're looking for our baby brother. He was kidnapped and dragged into this book, and we're here to rescue him. To do that we have to kill the Wicked Witch and get her broom for you, so why don't you do your little magic show so we can get on with it."

The head opened its mouth wide and Sabrina fully expected more complaints about respecting the plot, but instead she heard a deep, obnoxious belch.

The girls looked at each another in disbelief.

"I know that's not in the story," Daphne said.

The head laughed. "Why would I help a couple of monkey-faced freaks like you two?"

Sabrina glanced around the room. Standing not far from where they were was a tall green screen. She stepped over to it.

"Never mind the man behind the screen!" the head bellowed

as Sabrina pushed it aside. Standing behind it was a very familiar ragged-haired boy in a filthy green hoodie.

"Puck!" the girls cried.

On the floor next to him, tied tight with rope, was the Wizard. A green gag was shoved into his mouth and it was clear by his groans that he was not happy. Puck, however, looked as amused as Sabrina had ever seen him.

"Hello, Grimms," Puck said. "Are you having as much fun as I am?"

2

z rules!" Puck exclaimed.

"How did you get here?" Sabrina asked.

"After I stepped into that crazy book I was tossed inside a tornado. I got spun around at a million miles an hour and then was flung all the way to the Emerald City. It was awesome!"

Daphne looked down at the Wizard. His hands were bound tightly. "What's his story?"

"His guards found me and locked me in a cell," Puck said, giving the man a healthy kick in the rear. "The Wiz here figured out I was from the real world pretty fast and begged me to help him escape the Book."

"Escape the Book? Oh, dear," the Scarecrow murmured.

"That's what he said," Puck said. "I agreed to help, but knowing him like I do, I figured he would somehow double-cross me, so I decided to triple-cross him first. Then it dawned on me he might try a quadruple-cross so I immediately skipped the quindruple-, sexdruple-, and septdruple-, and went straight to the octdruple-cross. He never saw it coming! Once he turned his back, I tied him up and took over as the Great and Terrible Oz. The people either don't know the difference or don't care."

"Yeah, they keep treating me like I'm Dorothy," Daphne said.

"What about you?" Puck said, turning to Sabrina.

Sabrina's face turned bright red. "I'm Toto," she mumbled.

"Who?"

"I'm the dog! Are you satisfied?"

Puck burst into an obnoxious, horsey laugh. "I've been telling you that you were a dog since we first met. If we're getting married, you're going to have to go to the doctor and see what they can do about your face."

Sabrina seethed. "What are you talking about?"

"Us . . . getting married," Puck said. "You're my fiancée."

It took several moments for Puck's words to sink in. Puck couldn't have called her his "fiancée," could he? But the look on Daphne's face—an expression filled with thrills and romantic giggles—confirmed that her ears were not playing tricks. She was certain her own face was glowing as red as a stoplight.

"We're married in the future, right?" Puck continued. "You told me we were. At first the thought of marrying you made me sick. I mean, really physically ill. I was barfing and fevered. I spent a few days in bed with the chills, but then I realized, hey! Getting married might be the best thing that ever happened to me. I'll have someone to wait on me hand and foot. Having a wife is practically like having a slave, and I could really use the help. I hope you can cook, Grimm. I like to eat."

"A slave?!" Sabrina cried. "Is that what you think a wife is?"

"Of course," Puck said. "But before we get to that, we need to start planning our wedding and the reception. I was thinking we could have it in Pompeii, you know, where all those people were killed by the volcano—it's very romantic."

Sabrina thought she might explode like a volcano. She considered whether to strangle the boy now or in his sleep.

Daphne stepped between them. "We need you to fly us to the Wicked Witch's castle. We have to kill her and get her flying broom. We think it's our only way into the next story."

"Stop! STOP! STOP!!!!!!!" the Tin Man shouted. "You people don't understand what you are doing. You can't just skip ahead. Lots of stuff happens in between. The Editor will know!"

"Are they complaining about this Editor person too?" Puck said. "The Wizard was crying about him before I shoved the gag in his mouth. Personally, if I was going to terrorize people, I'd come up with a better name than the 'Editor.'"

"True, the 'Editor' is lousy as a scary name," Daphne said.

"Stop saying his name!" the Cowardly Lion whined.

"Do we have to take them?" Puck asked as his wings popped out of his back. They were pink and enormous, and with just a few flaps they lifted his body into the air.

"We'll finish the story on our own," the Tin Man said.

The Scarecrow and the Cowardly Lion nodded their heads in agreement.

"I have to warn you," Daphne said. "The Scarecrow has his hay yanked out, the Cowardly Lion is chained up in a yard, and the Tin Man is thrown out a window of the castle. You could all skip that stuff if you come with us."

"That's what happens to these guys?" Puck asked as he snatched the girls up. "You Grimms sure you don't want to go with them? It sounds hilarious."

Sabrina shook her head, and Puck flew the girls toward an open window. "Well, I wish I could say it was fun," Sabrina called back to the trio.

• • •

A second later, they were soaring high over the spiraling green towers of Emerald City. Heading due west, Puck's wings lifted them higher and higher until they could see nearly every mile of the Land of Oz. They flew on for the better part of an afternoon before a dark castle came into view.

Puck circled it once to find a good entrance and finally spotted an open window in a high tower. He swooped inside and they landed. The room was covered in tapestries the color of the night sky. In a far corner of the room, a dark figure was hovering over a crystal ball. Her face was illuminated by the ball's swirling light. Her skin was a pale shade of green. She had black, unkempt hair and a patch over her left eye. Her skin was covered in warts and her teeth were filed down into fangs. She was one of the scariest people Sabrina had ever seen, but when she noticed the children she let out a startled yelp and backed herself into the corner.

"You're early!" she cried. "You missed the flying-monkey attack! And the swarm of killer bees! I'm supposed to send all manner of torment against you before you get here."

"Sorry to disappoint you," Sabrina said, "but we have to move things along. Where do you keep the buckets of water?"

"Right. Right," the Witch said. She rushed across the room and returned with a bucket full of hot, soapy water and a mop, which she placed in front of Daphne. "Maybe the Editor won't even notice. OK, Dorothy, in this scene, you are scrubbing the floors. I'll go out and come back in, and when I do I'll be very angry. All you have to do is throw the water on me. Then I'll melt."

The Witch raced out into the hall.

"I don't want her to melt. I'll have nightmares," Daphne said.

"She's not real, Daphne," Sabrina said.

The Witch raced back into the room. She had a horrible expression on her face but it quickly changed to confusion. "Why aren't you scrubbing?"

"I don't want you to die," Daphne said.

"But that's what happened with the real Dorothy," the Witch said. "You have to make me melt. Don't worry about me! I've done it a million times. It doesn't even hurt that much anymore."

Daphne frowned. "It's not right."

Puck snatched the bucket from Daphne. "I would love to see her melt," he said.

Daphne snatched the bucket back. "No one is melting!"

"Give me back the bucket or you're not invited to the wedding," Puck cried.

"OK, everyone calm down," Sabrina said.

"Should I go back out and try this again?" the Witch asked.

"I won't do it," Daphne said.

"Daphne, we can't get to the door unless we do this," Sabrina said. "And we can't stay in this story. Mirror is in this book with our brother."

"I know that!" the little girl cried.

"Here, I'll make this easy on everyone. Give me the bucket," the Witch said and tried to snatch it from Daphne. "I'll pour it on myself."

"No!"

"Kid, let go of the bucket," the Witch demanded. "I want to melt! Really! I do!"

"You don't know what you want."

"I'm not kidding. Dump that water on me now."

"Forget it! You're staying dry!"

Just then, the Witch gave a mighty tug and the bucket fell onto her. Water splashed across her body and a hissing sound filled the room. The children could do nothing but watch as the woman's body began to dribble onto the floor like butter in a saucepan. A green puddle collected at their feet.

"Thank you *sooooo* much!" the Witch cried just before the smile on her face leaked down her dress.

Daphne was breathing deeply, and her face had taken on a queasy green hue that rivaled the Witch's complexion. "I am never going to get over that."

"I said it before and I'll say it again, Oz rules!" Puck cried.

Suddenly a door materialized out of thin air. Sabrina stepped over and circled around it. It was painted red and had a little brass knocker on it. It could have been the front door of a million different homes, only there was no physical reason the door should be standing in midair. But it was there, right in front of them, defying reason. Sabrina clasped the knob, turned it, and swung the door open. A blast of wind blew her hair, and all around her was a smell of a burning fireplace.

"So this takes us to the next story?" Puck shouted over the wind.

Sabrina nodded. "That's what we were told."

"Where do you think it leads to?" Daphne asked.

"I don't know, but I hope it isn't as annoying as Oz," Sabrina said.

"I hope it's a place where people don't melt," Daphne grumbled.

Sabrina took Daphne's and Puck's hands, and together they stepped through the door. There was a whooshing sound and Sabrina's stomach dropped, and then they suddenly found themselves in a somber library. All the furniture was a dark cherrywood. Tightly packed books, some that looked as old as time, were displayed neatly on bookshelves soaring hundreds of feet into the air. A yellowing globe sat on a stone podium, and the head of some horrible, alien animal was mounted above a crackling fireplace. In the center of the room was a high-backed leather chair, and resting in the chair was a thin, elderly man with hair as white as freshly fallen snow. A pair of antique spectacles sat precariously on the tip of his long, pointy nose. He leafed through a book with one hand and patted the bulbous head of a strange, pink creature with the other. Sabrina recognized it as one of the scurrying creatures that attacked them on the road in Oz—the one the Tin Man had called a "reviser." Its gnashing teeth and lack of eyes unnerved Sabrina.

"I know the fairy: Puck, Trickster, Imp, the Pooka," the old man said as he gestured to Puck. Then he turned his tiny eyes toward the girls. "You two I do not know."

"We're Sabrina and Daphne Grimm," Sabrina said.

"Did you say 'Grimm'?"

"Yes, sir. What story is this?" Daphne asked.

Sabrina looked down at her own clothes to see if she and her sister had new outfits, but both she and Daphne were wearing their own clothing again. Even the silver slippers were gone. She looked up and saw that Dorothy's shoes were resting on a tray. The old man placed them in the mouth of the reviser next to his chair.

"Prepare these for reinsertion into the story," he said, and

then turned his attention back to the children. "You are not in a story. You are in my library—a place few humans or Everafters have ever seen. I have been forced to bring you here to protect the sanctity of the Book you and your comrades are sullying. Running around in my pages causes quite a bit of damage."

"You're the Editor," Sabrina said.

Four more of the pink creatures crawled out from beneath the old man's chair. He treated them like pets, scratching affectionately at their grotesque heads and bellies. "The characters in the Book of Everafter are difficult enough to manage without the interference of visitors. You've made a complete mess out of *The Wonderful Wizard of Oz*. You skipped over parts, you butchered the dialogue, and you changed the climax. I don't remember the Witch begging Dorothy to kill her. My revisers will have quite a bit of work ahead of them to put things back to the way they really happened."

The old man rose from his chair and crossed the room to the door the children had just stepped through, which was still standing open in the middle of the floor. The pink monsters followed him there, and when he knelt down they grinned and squeaked. He waved a hand as if to calm them and then spoke softly.

"I'm afraid I need more than the five of you," he said. "I'm thinking *The Wonderful Wizard of Oz* needs a complete page-one rewrite. We're going to start over with this one. No use discovering we have a problem later."

The little pink monsters hopped forward to lick the man's hand with their long, white tongues and then scurried back. To Sabrina's amazement, the five divided themselves into ten, then twenty, then forty, and on and on and on. They were like bacteria in a petri dish, reproducing at an alarming rate, until there were hundreds of them. They scuttled through the open doorway with their huge, fanged mouths open wide, and then the doorway closed.

"What are they going to do?" Daphne asked.

"They are revisers, child. They are going to fix the changes you have made—which have been numerous."

"And how do they do that?" Sabrina asked suspiciously.

"They're going to erase everyone and everything."

"Erase?"

"I suppose a more accurate word would be 'eat.'"

"Those things are going to eat everyone we met in Oz? Because of us?" Daphne cried.

"Can I watch?" Puck said.

"That's what a reviser does," the Editor said. "When they are finished, I can re-craft the story so that it matches what happened at the actual event. You seem troubled, but if I were to allow the changes you made to stay in place . . . well, it would change history—real history. Dorothy might have been trapped in Oz for good. The repercussions could be unpredictable and dangerous. Luckily, I'm here to put it back the way it has always been."

"I have no idea what you're talking about," Sabrina said.

The Editor sighed impatiently. "Just like a Grimm to leap into a magic book without knowing how it works. Let me explain this in simple terms. A hundred years ago the Book of Everafter was created by the Everafter community as a sort of history book of its people—a living, breathing diorama of the places and events cherished most by the fairy-tale folk of Ferryport Landing. Many of the stories mirror those documented by Jacob and Wilhelm Grimm, L. Frank Baum, Hans Christian Andersen, et cetera, but unlike the writings of those men, a person can actually walk into this history book and interact with the characters. This provided the community with the opportunity to vacation away from the town and its barrier, if they so desired—reliving their glory days, as it were. For nearly four decades, it was enjoyed by many, until an Everafter abused the privilege and altered the magic for her own personal gain. She turned the Book's magic into something its original creators never imagined."

"What did she do?" Daphne cried.

"She linked it to real history."

"Huh?" Puck said.

"Pay attention!" the Editor snapped. "The changes she made were very dangerous. Now when someone steps into the Book of Everafter, they can choose to change things they don't like, and history, in the real world, is forever changed. They can marry a different princess, choose not to kiss a frog, or arrive in time to make sure the Wolf does not eat their grandmother. Whatever they change in these stories will change history. The real world will bend and twist to fit the changes. No one will remember that anything is different. This Everafter did just that—she went into her story, caused havoc, and her changes changed history."

"Who was it?" Daphne asked.

"That is privileged information. All I will say is that her tale was tragic and heartbreaking and now, it is not. Needless to say, the woman made a mess and couldn't put the story back together in a way that made any sense. So she created me, and the revisers, to help her fill in the holes. Since then, it has become my duty to clean up any further changes made by visitors, and to keep the status quo. But you fools are messing things up. Every little change you make changes reality—that is, if I don't fix it back before it's too late."

"We didn't know!" Daphne cried.

"Clearly," the Editor said.

Sabrina scowled. "We're not a bunch of meddlesome kids joyriding in your stupid book. We're trying to rescue a member of our family. Once we find him, we'll go."

The Editor frowned as he sat back in his big chair. "I can feel his presence, as well as two others—the Magic Mirror, and Pinocchio, the marionette who wished to be a real boy."

"Pinocchio helped Mirror kidnap our brother," Daphne said.

"Regardless of their real-world transgressions, you do not belong here." The old man gestured to the other side of the room and another doorway materialized. The door swung open. On the other side stood Granny Relda and the girls' parents in the Hall of Wonders, looking down into the Book of Everafter. From their confused expressions, Sabrina could tell they couldn't see the girls or the library in which they were standing.

Sabrina considered the Editor's explanation. Perhaps one of the adults might do a better job than she would. If she went back, her mother or father could step in and take up the hunt. Granny Relda would know what to do. The temptation to let someone else make the big choices was incredible.

"We're not going without our brother," Daphne said, jarring her sister from her conflicted thoughts. "Mirror is planning on stealing his body. We won't go until he's safe. I don't care if we wreck every story in this book."

The Editor shifted in his chair. His face showed anger and surprise. "Leave now or my revisers will devour you," he seethed.

Puck shrugged. "I've been eaten before. It's no big deal."

Daphne pulled Puck and Sabrina back toward the doorway they and the revisers had just stepped through. She opened it and faced a terrible wind layered with heat and humidity, and smelling like something untamed and dangerous.

"You are making a terrible mistake!" the Editor shouted over the sound of the wind.

"If I had a nickel for every time a bad guy told me that, I'd be a rich detective," Daphne said. She pushed everyone through, and suddenly there was a stomach-dropping moment, and then the Editor and his creepy pets were gone.

• • •

Sabrina stood on a large, flat rock beneath an inky night sky. The air was hot and humid and heavy with the musk of wild creatures. Jungle trees dipped down overheard and the full moon's light lit up the ground. In her hand was a torch, which she held above her head. Its light revealed savage beasts surrounding her—a pack of wolves. Each held its haunches high, but their eyes were on the ground and many were trembling in fear. The torch also illuminated the dirty loincloth that barely covered her.

"Thou art the master," a voice said from the trees above her head. It was smooth and serious, and when she looked up at it she realized its owner was a black panther nestled in the branches. "Save Akela from the death. He was ever your friend."

Terrified, Sabrina screamed and stumbled backward. When the panther did not pounce, she tried to calm herself. She told herself over and over again that she was in a story and story animals were not the same as their man-eating real-life versions. At least, she hoped they weren't. The fact that the panther was talking boded well too. Most of the talking animals in Ferryport Landing weren't savage—annoying for sure, but not blood-thirsty. Still, there was no sign of Daphne or Puck. Perhaps they had been the appetizers and she was about to become the main course. "Daphne? Puck? I could really use some help here."

An old gray wolf stood nearby, its head bowed in obedience. When she spoke, he looked up in confusion. "What did the man-cub say?"

"I have no idea," another said.

"Could the man-cub repeat what he just said?"

"Man-cub?" Sabrina said, confused.

Then a figure on hands and knees crawled toward her. It was Daphne and she was giggling. "We're in *The Jungle Book!*"

Sabrina had not read *The Jungle Book*. Granny Relda had told her that its main character, Mowgli, was a good kid, so she had flipped through the book quickly and moved on to the next. Looking back, that hadn't been the best strategy.

"I'm a wolf," Daphne said, letting out a goofy howl at the silver moon. It sounded less like a wolf and more like a wounded house cat. "Guess who you are! You're Mowgli!"

Sabrina searched her memory for facts about Mowgli. He was a boy from India who was raised by wolves—he had a friend that was a sloth bear and another that was a panther. She seemed to recall there was something else about a tiger, but she couldn't remember anything specific. Was the tiger really annoying and bouncing around a lot? Maybe that was another story.

"Where's Puck?" Sabrina asked.

Daphne shrugged as she got to her feet. "He's around here somewhere."

Sabrina frowned as she studied the wolf pack nervously. "Any idea what we're supposed to do before we're turned into dog food?"

"Pardon me?" one of the wolves cried. "We are not dogs. We are wolves!"

"Proud ones at that!" another shouted.

Just then, a huge animal lumbered onto the rock. It was orange and white and all muscle. Sabrina nearly dropped her torch in fright when she realized it was a Bengal tiger. This particular animal hobbled on a lame foot, but that did nothing to detract from its menacing presence.

"Enough!" it roared. "This is not how things went. You are supposed to grant Akela a pardon from the death and then accept your banishment from the pack and the Council. Then you are supposed to attack some of the wolves with your torch and then attack me. You must stick to what happened, or the revisers will come. Follow the original events or I will kill you where you stand, man-cub."

"First, I'm not a 'man-cub.' If anything I'm a woman-cub," Sabrina said. "Secondly, I don't know this story well enough to follow it, so you're going to have cut me a break."

"Perhaps I should just cut you," Shere Khan said, flashing the claws on his good paw.

A figure dropped out of the sky and landed between the girls and the tiger. "Keep your paws off my fiancée, you flea-ridden stray," Puck shouted.

"By the lock that freed me," the panther cried as he craned his neck to eye the boy fairy. "Who are you?"

Puck put his hands on his hips and puffed up his chest. "I am the Trickster King. Leader of the Lazy, Master of Mayhem, Savior of the—surely you've heard of me."

The wolves looked at one another and then shook their heads. "Are you one of the monkey people?"

Puck frowned and turned back toward Shere Khan. "No, I am not one of the monkey people. I am the sworn protector of the Grimms and you will not touch them, or I will turn the hose on you."

Shere Khan roared so powerfully that Puck's hair was blown into an even bigger mess than usual.

"We're in *The Jungle Book*," Daphne said to Puck. "They think Sabrina is Mowgli and I'm one of the wolves."

"Whoever you are, you are messing with the story!" Shere Khan bellowed. A strand of saliva leaked out of the creature's mouth and dribbled to the ground. "The Editor will not tolerate it, and I have no intention of being revised."

"What are you going to do about it?" Puck taunted. "Go ahead, raise your paw to me. I need a new rug."

The tiger leaped forward with every talon extended. He slashed at the boy fairy, who barely had time to pull his wooden sword from his pants and block the mighty blow. Puck swung back but his tiny weapon was deflected by a vicious swat. The sword flew out of his hand and landed in some tall grass. Shere Khan's razor-sharp claws caught the side of Puck's hoodie and slashed it to ribbons. Puck yelped as his wings extended and he flew into the air.

"Puck!" Sabrina cried.

As he hovered above the tiger, Puck looked slightly rattled, but he gestured for the girls to stay where they were. "It's OK. I shouldn't have underestimated him. He may not be real, but his claws are."

"Come down here, mosquito, so I can finish the job," Shere Khan said.

Puck swooped down and snatched his sword from the grass. Then he flew directly over the tiger and swung his weapon into Shere Khan's spine. The huge cat groaned in agony and fell to the ground.

"If I were you I'd slink back to your owner," Puck said. "Perhaps you'll get a bowl of milk."

Shere Khan lumbered to his feet. His bright orange hide glowed in the firelight and his eyes smoldered like hot coals. He glared at Puck, and then in one sudden movement he leaped toward a tree and used it to launch himself at his enemy. Puck kicked him in the face, but not before the creature slashed at his chest. The deadly claws had only missed his skin by a fraction of an inch. Puck's hoodie would never be the same.

Sabrina was shaken. Like Puck, she too had assumed they couldn't be hurt in the stories. They weren't actually the people they were pretending to be. They were more like actors playing the parts in the stories. She would never have suspected that they would ever really be attacked. She had once been in a school production of *Stone Soup* in the second grade and none of the pilgrims had attacked her. The risk of injury or death added another worry to her rapidly growing list of concerns.

Puck lunged at the beast again, but it smacked him backward with a well-timed punch. He fell from the sky and rolled into Sabrina, knocking the torch out of her grasp. It fell onto the flat, smooth rock and rolled into an outcrop of tall grass nearby. A moment later, the wild flora burst into hungry flames that threatened to spread to everything around it.

"What have you done?" the black panther cried.

"What have I done?" Sabrina repeated. "The tiger is the one causing the problems!"

An old wolf stepped forward to address the other wolves. "Flee, brothers. The red flower is blossoming." The wolves howled and darted into the burning jungle. The black panther leaped down from his tree and followed them in a panic.

"What red flower?" Sabrina said.

"They're talking about the fire," Daphne said. "It's part of the book, but this forest fire is not. The story wouldn't have been very good if Mowgli torched the forest and killed everything for miles."

"Speak for yourself," Puck said, still fighting with the tiger. "That story would rule."

"What should we do?" Sabrina asked.

"We need to get out of here!" Daphne shouted.

"Right behind you," Puck said.

The girls started to follow the fleeing pack but were stopped in their tracks by Shere Khan. His eyes locked onto the children and his jaws filled with angry foam. Sabrina couldn't tell whether the rising temperature she felt came from the fire or the rage wafting off the jungle cat.

"You have doomed us all. The Editor and his revisers will be here any moment," Shere Khan said. "Perhaps he will spare me if I kill those responsible for the damage."

Puck zipped down and snatched each of the girls by the back of their shirts. A moment later, they were rising skyward. "If Garfield the cat here won't let us pass, I suppose we'll have to take another route."

Shere Khan leaped at them, swatting with his massive paws, but the children were already out of his reach and sailing over the fiery jungle.

"Thanks for the save," Sabrina said.

"No problem, honey bunny," Puck said. "I can't exactly let my bride-to-be become cat food."

"The second we're on the ground, I'm going to put my fist into your mouth, you stinky, scummy sack of stupid," Sabrina said.

Just then, a stone sailed into the air and slammed into Puck's head. "Owww!" he cried, flapping awkwardly in the air and nearly dropping the girls. Sabrina looked down and saw hundreds of monkeys swinging from treetops and shaking angry fists at them.

"I think those are the monkey people we heard about," Daphne said.

Puck did his best to avoid the flying rocks, zigging and zagging around each projectile, but there were too many of them. Their only defense was to fly higher.

"How does this story end?" Sabrina asked. "We can't stay up here much longer."

"That depends," Daphne said. "*The Jungle Book* is a collection of short stories. Technically, this part is over, and so the door might be down there."

"You want me to fly down into that inferno?" Puck said.

"Yes?" Sabrina squeaked. She hoped her uncertainty was covered by the wind.

"You're completely insane—a good quality in a wife. Hold on," Puck said. His wings stopped flapping and the three dropped toward the ground. Sabrina was sure they were about to be splattered on the jungle floor when Puck's wings expanded and caught an updraft of hot air. They glided to safety and touched down on the ground, surrounded by burning trees.

"Do you see a door?" Daphne asked as she scanned their surroundings.

"It could be anywhere," Puck said.

Sabrina began to panic. Puck was right. She hadn't read *The Jungle Book* from cover to cover, but she remembered lots of settings—the Council Rock, the human village, the giant snake's lair—the door to the next story could be anywhere. Maybe they should have stayed in the sky. Maybe they would have been able to see it from up there.

She wondered how things could possibly get any worse when she got her answer. From out of the trees stampeded a herd of long-horned cattle. They tore through the jungle, their hooves grinding everything into pulp and their horns goring trees and bushes. Their panicked bellows rose above the noise of the roaring and crackling fire. The children leaped behind some ancient trees for protection, but unfortunately, another wave of cattle was approaching from that direction as well. Nowhere was safe.

"Don't worry, honey," Puck said to Sabrina. He spun around on his heels and she watched him hulk up in a disturbing transformation. One of Puck's many abilities as a fairy was to change into a variety of different animals, which didn't make it any less weird each time he did it. His arms grew in length and his shoulders hunched with dense muscles. As his whole body sprouted thick, black fur, Sabrina could tell he was transforming into a gorilla. He snatched the girls in his huge arms, climbed a tree, and plopped them all onto a high branch. A moment later he morphed back to his true form.

"We'll be safe here," Puck said as they eyed the sea of cattle below.

"Are you sure?" Daphne said. "Look!"

From within the stampede, Sabrina spotted a herd of creatures altogether unlike the cows. These were small, pink, and fast, with little legs and arms to scurry along the ground.

"Revisers!" Sabrina cried.

Everything that got in the way of the revisers was quickly devoured and vanished. In fact, the very jungle was disappearing—every inch was being replaced with an empty, white void.

"I vote that we get out of here!" Daphne shouted.

"I second that," Sabrina said.

Puck's wings unfolded and he grabbed the girls. Soon the trio was zipping along the tree line, high above the hungry monsters, but Sabrina felt far from safe. The entire world was vanishing, not just the trees and animals—even the night sky was being devoured. Each of the little pink creatures was an eating machine, chomping on the cattle, the trees, the ground, everything. The Editor's words echoed in her mind.

Leave now or my revisers will devour you.

Daphne's eyes were wide with fear. "They're very fast."

"Don't worry. I'm faster!" Puck shouted. "Besides, would I let something happen to my fiancée and my future sister-in-law? While we're on the subject, I was hoping we could discuss our wedding cake. I'd like to go traditional—you know, something stuffed with wild boar and drizzled with spider icing. What do you think, honey? Oh, and when do you want to go and look at engagement rings?"

Sabrina wondered if it would be better to shake herself loose and die on the jungle floor rather than take more of the stinky boy's teasing. "You keep flapping your mouth, fairy, and I'm going to engage my fist to your lip."

Just then, Puck's body jerked to a sudden stop. All three of the children fell like stones. They landed hard on the ground and lay there for a moment, groaning in pain. Sharp agony raced along Sabrina's hip and another pain ached in her right shoulder.

"I didn't see that branch," Puck said.

"Branch? It felt like a truck to me," Daphne said as she crawled to her feet.

Sabrina sat up, nursing her wounds. She was sure her whole left side would be black-and-blue in the morning. "We have to keep moving."

The three helped one another up and began to stagger forward. There was no path to follow and the exposed roots and heavy brush did not make walking easy. Before long, Sabrina could hear the hungry, chattering teeth of the Editor's pets behind her. She turned and spotted one darting in the undergrowth several yards behind them.

How could she have chased after Mirror into this crazy book? She had signed their death warrant because she had made another dumb mistake . . .

"There's the door!" Daphne shouted.

Sabrina peered into the brush. Something white was standing in the bushes up ahead—something that didn't belong there. Daphne was right! There was a door, but could they reach it before the revisers devoured them? She dug deep into herself and found the energy to run harder and faster. Her determination to save her family and herself made the pain in her hips and legs vanish.

Before she knew it, she was turning the knob and opening the door. Daphne and Puck tumbled through and Sabrina started to follow. Before she could, a reviser clamped down on her loincloth. It growled and tore at the cloth. Sabrina could feel its incredible strength as it pulled her back with its teeth, and she fell to the ground. It dragged her away along the ground toward the hungry jaws of the rest of its pack. She kicked at the creature, pounding it with her feet, but nothing could stop it.

She was sure she was about to die when the creature let go of her loincloth and was lifted off the ground. It squirmed and cried as if in the hold of a viselike grip, but there was no one there holding it up. Sabrina didn't stop to figure it out. She scurried backward into the open doorway.

Just before the jungle vanished from view, she saw the reviser slam into the ground. It looked as if it were dead. She remembered the Munchkin's warnings about staying inside the margins. Was this invisible power what he was trying to tell her about?

3

hen the world materialized again, Sabrina found
herself at the edge of another unfamiliar, dark
forest. Unlike the setting of the fierce and fiery
Jungle Book, this one smelled of cedar pines, and a layer of
crisp dew covered everything. The change of scenery wasn't the
only thing that was different. She and Daphne were dressed
in new outfits—puffy shirts and royal blue leggings. Sabrina
sighed in relief. Anything was better than the loincloth she had
been wearing. Puck was still in his usual filthy and shredded
hoodie. She guessed that as an Everafter, he was allowed to
stroll through the Book unaltered. Perhaps the Book, like the
Editor, recognized Puck. Because the girls were human, they
were unfamiliar. Maybe that's why it kept forcing them into
different roles.

Her little sister seemed thrilled with her new attire. She had discovered a sharp sword sheathed at her side. She took it out and awkwardly swung it around. "Maybe we're in *The Three Musketeers*! I hope I'm D'Artagnan. Hey, that's a good name for the baby. D'Artagnan Grimm."

Daphne swung her sword into a nearby tree, where it stuck tight. As she struggled to pry it loose, Sabrina glanced around and saw they were traveling with a crowd of similarly dressed men. Each had long, shoulder-length hair and a full beard. Leading the group along a well-worn path through the trees was a woman in rich, embroidered robes. A golden crown adorned with delicate jewels rested on her head. Her face, however, was not as delicate. It was a collection of sharp features and rough lines—both gorgeous and unnerving. Sabrina feared her smile more than any weapon.

"Which story is this?" Puck asked.

Daphne shrugged. "Beats me."

Sabrina was disappointed. Daphne had read so many more fairy tales than she had, and even though Sabrina had accepted her role as a fairy-tale detective, there weren't enough hours in the day to read and memorize every fable, tall tale, and folk story in the family's private library. It was at moments like this that she wished she hadn't been so stubbornly resistant when Granny Relda had explained her family history and responsibilities. If she had been more cooperative and listened more closely, she might know more about the stories and the actual historical events they described.

"What is it with all the forests?" Daphne grumbled as she peered into the woods.

"I know! Couldn't they set one of these stories in an ice-cream parlor for once? I'm starving!" Puck exclaimed. His outburst stopped the rest of the group in their tracks. Every eye shot angry daggers at the children.

"No one spoke during this part," one of the guards whispered.

They followed the group quietly until they came to an overgrown part of the path, so faint it would have been easy to overlook it. The queen held her hand up, and her men came to an abrupt stop. As everyone looked on, the queen reached into the folds of her robes and took out a ball of white yarn. Sabrina wondered if the woman was planning on knitting a scarf when she saw the queen do something unexpected. She raised the ball of yarn to her mouth and whispered something into it. Then she set it on the ground at her feet and stood back. The ball of yarn started to twitch and hop. It bounced around like a Mexican jumping bean and then rolled into the woods with a shot, leaving in its wake a strand of yarn for them to follow.

The queen reached down and snatched the loose end of yarn

and began to wrap it into a new ball as she followed the string into the woods.

"Ahhh, now I know where we are," Daphne said. "This is one that Jacob and Wilhelm wrote about. It's called 'The Six Swans.'"

Sabrina had a vague memory of reading it, or rather, of struggling to stay awake while she read it. Clearly, she had lost the battle.

"That woman is a witch. Her husband is a king and he has seven children with his first wife. The queen wants to do bad things to his kids, so the king hides them in a cabin in the woods. She's using a ball of magic yarn that will unroll until it takes her to where they are."

"So the yarn is like a GPS device or something?" Sabrina asked.

A guard shot them an angry look. "Shhhhh!"

"Yes," Daphne whispered. "In the story I read, it leads her to their cabin."

The children trudged through the dense woods for the next hour. The men followed the queen obediently as she collected and wrapped her ball of yarn. Finally they came to a cottage built near a bubbling spring. Six smiling boys, the oldest not much older than Sabrina, raced out of the cabin toward the group. Their eyes were bright with joy until they saw the queen. When they turned to flee, the men pounced on them and dragged them to the wicked stepmother. From the folds of her dress she removed six silk shirts, and one by one she pulled them over the heads of the boys. In a flash of light, each boy made what appeared to be a painful, squawking transformation into a white swan. Legs and arms vanished. Lean bodies turned plump and sprouted feathers. Toes were replaced with webbed feet. Once each of the boys had changed, the queen's men released the swans. The distraught gaggle took to the air and disappeared over the treetops.

"She turned them into birds!" Sabrina said. It hadn't been long ago that she had been turned into a goose, and sometimes she still felt the instinct to shove her head into the river and feast on tiny fish. "What happens to them next?"

"I don't remember everything, but I think their sister finds a way to break the spell," Daphne said. "But to do it she has to keep quiet for six years."

"What did you say?" the queen asked.

The girls turned to see the queen standing behind them, listening to every word.

"Did you say the king has another child?" she continued.

"Um," Daphne said.

"I'm not supposed to know that! Now it's part of the story. I have to go in there and turn her into a swan too. If I don't, my motivations won't make any sense, but if I do, how will the boys get rescued?"

"You could pretend you didn't hear it," Sabrina suggested.

The queen shook her head. "Guards, these three children have brought the Editor to our story. The revisers will be here at any moment."

At the word "revisers," the guards raced into the woods as if running for their lives. The queen followed them, dropping her end of the ball of yarn in her flight.

"We're sorry!" Daphne shouted to them.

"Messing up these stories is kind of fun," Puck said. "I hope we run into Ms. Muffet. I'll give her something to be afraid of . . ."

Sabrina's gaze fell on the queen's ball of yarn. She snatched it up and immediately felt the uncomfortable sensation she always experienced when handling magical items. If she held it for too long, she'd be overcome with the urge to use it. So she shoved it into her sister's hand.

"Wow! The magic in this thing is strong, even more than Dorothy's slippers. Let's give it a try," Daphne said as she held the yarn ball to her mouth. "Take us to Mirror."

At once, the ball of yarn fell out of the young girl's hands and rolled into the woods. Sabrina watched it with amazement. "Is it possible? Could it really take us to him and our baby brother?"

Daphne shrugged. "Only one way to find out."

The children chased the rolling ball of yarn through the woods, collecting the loose strand and re-wrapping it as they went. The faster they ran, the faster the yarn seemed to roll, until it zipped down a small embankment to a dry creek bed, where a door materialized. The ball of yarn stopped in front of the door and hopped around as if eager to keep moving.

"So there are doors inside the stories." Sabrina smiled. "We can stop worrying about going all the way to the end before we find one."

It seemed as if something was finally going their way. She opened the door and the wind that came out smelled like burning wood and leather. It was oddly familiar. The yarn rolled forward into the void and disappeared. Sabrina took her sister by the hand and snatched Puck by the collar and together they followed the yarn.

The first thing Sabrina heard was a crackling fire and the sound of someone flipping through the dry pages of an old book. When she blinked, she found herself lying on her back in the Editor's library. Above her, sitting in his leather chair, was the man himself. He looked down and cocked a curious eyebrow.

Sabrina scampered to her feet and prepared to fight.

"Calm down," the Editor said.

"You sent those monsters to eat us," Sabrina said. She helped Daphne to her feet. Puck was already behind her.

"If that were true, why would I send a door and bring you here?"

"Maybe you want to try and kill us yourself," Puck said.

The Editor sighed. "I do not want the three of you dead. I want to hire you."

The trio stared incredulously at one another as the Editor got up from his seat and poked at some dying embers in his fireplace. A dozen of his revisers scurried out from underneath his chair and scuttled across the floor. They clambered up the shelves like fat spiders and seemed to melt into the shadows on the far-distant ceiling.

"You want to hire us?" Sabrina said.

The Editor placed his hands together and lightly tapped his fingers as if in serious thought. "You are detectives, correct? The last member of your family I had in my book claimed it was a family business."

"Excuse me?"

"The one who called herself Trixie Grimm," he said.

"Great-Aunt Trixie," Daphne said. "She was Grandpa Basil's sister-in-law."

"I find myself in a most peculiar situation that requires your kind of skills," he said.

"What do you want us to do?" Sabrina asked.

"I want you to find a missing person," the Editor said. "Detectives do such work all the time."

"A missing person? Who?" Sabrina asked suspiciously.

"Pinocchio," the thin man said as his face tightened into a scowl.

"Pinocchio! I almost forgot he was here," Daphne said. "He jumped into this book right before we did."

"And not unlike the three of you, he is causing a great deal of trouble for the Book," the Editor replied. "While you three are running through one story, he's causing mayhem in another. I've been working overtime trying to make sure these stories are put back the way they were meant to be before they can change history. Then it dawned on me—why not hire you three to chase him?"

"How does that help you?" Daphne asked warily.

"Setting you on Pinocchio's trail will mean that all four of you will be in the same stories at the same time, cutting my work in half. Plus, you can help me prevent the boy from reaching his ultimate goal, which is to change his history."

"What does it matter, really?" Sabrina asked. "Anything Pinocchio changes you can rewrite with your little pink monsters."

The Editor shook his head. "The revisers work like white blood cells, seeking out an infection in the body. In this case, the Book is the body and you intruders are the infection. Unfortunately, they won't recognize him as a problem if he finds his way to his story—in some ways he belongs there. They won't be able to tell what's wrong and what's meant to be. They'll erase everything but what he changes, so I'll have to rebuild a new story around his alterations. I fear that despite the best intentions of the Everafter who used magic to manipulate this book, the spell isn't foolproof. Certain deleted elements struggle to make it back into her story. The slightest change could cause the whole tale to fall apart. Who knows what could happen in the real world."

"We're not interested in your offer," Sabrina said. "While we're hunting down that little traitor, Mirror might get to his story—and if what you're saying is true, he can make whatever changes he likes in his story and there's nothing the revisers can do. We can't risk missing our chance to stop him."

"Don't be so hasty, sugar bear," Puck said with a devilish grin. "He wants to hire us. We could use that money for the wedding. Ice sculptures of minotaurs and cyclopes are not cheap! Plus, don't forget about the poison ivy for your bouquet."

Sabrina scowled.

"I can assure you Mirror will never reach his story," the Editor said. "His particular story is off-limits, bound by powerful magics few could break. He will never attain whatever goal he has, thus you three have all the time in the world to find the puppet for me. Afterward, I will take you to Mirror and help retrieve your brother."

Daphne said. "Is Mirror's story the one that's falling apart? Is that the story the Everafter altered to change her history?"

"That is none of your concern. Do we have a deal?"

Sabrina looked to her sister. "What do you think?"

"If what he says is true and Mirror can't change his story, I think we can help. It would be nice to not have to worry about those things anymore," Daphne said, pointing to one of the pink monsters hovering by the Editor's leg.

"Children, my revisers are beautiful creatures, but they are not immensely intelligent," the Editor said. "They will eat everything they can get their teeth into. If you see one, it would be advisable to run in the opposite direction."

"So you can't stop them?"

The Editor shook his head. "When an intruder makes a change, I open a door and send them through. When they get to their destination, they do things their way."

Daphne and Puck looked to Sabrina for guidance, but she felt too paralyzed to make a decision. Having the Editor's help with Mirror could be just what they needed to stop him, but could they trust the Editor? She used to think she could read people, but now she wasn't so sure. What if he was leading them on a wild-goose chase?

"I'm in," Puck said, interrupting her thoughts. "If it gives me a chance to punch Pinocchio in his stupid, pointy nose, then I'm all for it."

Daphne nodded. "He should be easy to find, too. We know he's eager to change his past. He wants to convince the Blue Fairy to let him grow up. We snatch the little toad before he changes the story and bring him back here. Sounds like a piece of cake."

"And you swear you will help us stop Mirror?" Sabrina said. She eyed the strange man closely. She wanted him to see her gaze. She wanted him to feel as if she could see through him.

"You have my word," the Editor said. "Stop Pinocchio and I will do everything in my power to help you with the magic mirror and the boy."

The Editor waved his hand and a door appeared. With another wave, the door opened and a gust of wind blasted Sabrina's hair into her face. The air was sweaty and pungent, like a landmark case of bad personal hygiene.

"Use the ball of yarn to move quickly through the stories," the Editor said, handing it back to the little girl. "When you find our enemy, shout for me. I can hear you and open a door. Don't forget his annoying marionettes, either. They are just as damaging to the Book as their master."

"We'll do our best," Daphne said.

"I'm confident. One last thing. The Munchkin told you to stay inside the margins of the story, and he was correct. Don't run about in the parts that aren't in the tale. The margins are filled with loose memories and things that have been forgotten by history. Something lives there that you do not want to encounter. You experienced it, didn't you, Sabrina?"

Sabrina nodded. Something had grabbed that reviser in *The Jungle Book*—something she could not see.

"The invisible thing that killed my reviser will do the same to you if it gets a chance. Stay inside the events of the story," the Editor said. His face was grave with worry.

• • •

On the other side of the door, Sabrina found herself sitting in a milky fog. As she turned to look around, the fog danced and swirled. There was so much of the stuff that she could barely see her hand in front of her, but it was quiet and the fog was beautiful so she took a moment to calm her nerves.

When her breathing slowed and her heart stopped threatening to pound out of her chest, she stood up and looked at her new surroundings. She had never seen anything like it. The fog was thick and came up to her kneecaps. It glided around with the slightest movement or breath. There was nothing else but crystal blue sky as far as she could see. The ground beneath her was strange as well. It felt spongy, like she was standing on a giant slice of angel food cake.

"Uh, are we in heaven?" Daphne said, sitting up in the fog.

"No chance," Puck answered. "I highly doubt they would let me in."

They got to their feet and joined Sabrina, bouncing on the mushy ground beneath them.

"It's like we're walking around on someone's belly," Puck said.

Knowing Puck's joke was completely possible, Sabrina snatched her sister's hand and pulled her to her side. "Stay close."

Daphne shrugged. "It's more like I'm walking on the moon. This is one small step for man, one giant leap for Daphne."

"Cool it!" Sabrina said. "The less attention we draw to ourselves, the better off we'll be."

The little girl jumped one last time and came down with a jingle. "Ouch!"

"What happened?"

"I just landed on something," she said. Daphne reached down into the fog and pulled up the end of a heavy burlap sack tied with twine. She untied it, dipped her hands inside, and pulled out a fistful of gold coins.

"We're rich!" Puck said. "I say if we have to be stuck in this book, we should at least get to keep the treasure we find. We'll use it for our wedding reception, dear."

Sabrina turned pink and struggled to come up with a suitable insult.

Puck bent over and farted, then scratched his rear. "I'm no detective, but I'm sure that bag is a clue."

"And all this fog?" Daphne added. "Does any of this sound familiar?"

Just then, there was an enormous crash and the ground shifted, and all three of them toppled over like bowling pins.

"What was that?" Puck cried, but his words were drowned by another monstrous thud and shake.

"I don't think we should stick around to find out," Sabrina said.

As they helped one another up, an angry bellow filled their ears. It sounded almost human, only it was louder than anything the children had ever heard. The hair on Sabrina's arms stood at attention and shivers raced along her spine.

"OK, we can relax," Puck said. A grin spread across his face.

"Relax? What about all that noise?" Daphne asked.

"You didn't hear what he said?" Puck said.

"He? All I heard was a roar," Sabrina said.

"Nope, those were words."

"Well, what did he say?" Sabrina said just as another thud rocked the ground. This time the children managed to keep their balance, but just barely.

"He said, 'Fe, fi, fo, fum.'"

Fear rose up in Sabrina's throat like a bad shrimp. She knew what kind of monsters said "fe, fi, fo, fum." Giants! She'd met about a hundred of them her second day in Ferryport Landing. And she and her family had nearly been killed.

"We're not standing in fog," Daphne said. "We're standing on a cloud."

"Run!" Sabrina shouted, and they all took off at a sprint just as a shoe the size of a battleship came crashing down. If the children had stayed just one second longer, they would have been squished into paste by the creature's heel.

Sabrina scanned the horizon and spotted the top of an enormous beanstalk breaking through the clouds. She recalled the famous tale of Jack, who traded the family's cow for magic beans that grew into a giant beanstalk overnight. "There!" she said, steering the group across the challenging terrain.

"Who's that?" Daphne said, pointing toward the mutated plant.

Sabrina strained her eyes and saw a lone figure making his way down the beanstalk. He couldn't have been taller than three feet high and wore bright blue overalls. He also had a pointy nose and a terrible overbite. "Pinocchio!" she cried.

The little boy must have heard her, as he redoubled his efforts to escape. Sabrina took a deep breath and ran faster than she ever had before. The boy had betrayed her and her family. They had taken him into their lives, protected him, given him a home and a community, but the whole time he had been working for Mirror and the Scarlet Hand.

When the children reached the beanstalk, Sabrina could no longer see her target. He had climbed down the enormous plant, which sunk into the misty clouds below. Sabrina grabbed on to a thick leaf and was surprised to find it so sticky. She realized that was a good thing—perhaps it would save them all from slipping or taking a foolish step out into nothingness. She lowered herself to the next leaf, then the next. Daphne followed, then Puck, and soon the three were steadily descending from the giant's realm and into the open air. Far below there was a tiny cottage on an overgrown farm, but staring at it made Sabrina's belly turn inside out. She had never been afraid of heights, but then again she had never been up that high.

"Don't look down!" she cried.

"Then how are we going to see *them*?" Daphne said as she pointed down the beanstalk. Crawling up toward them at amazing speed were six wooden marionettes, each carved by a brilliant hand to look like members of Sabrina's family: Granny Relda, Dad, Mom, Uncle Jake, Daphne, and Sabrina. They leaped from leaf to leaf like monkeys. When they reached the children, they attacked viciously with little hands and feet. Despite their size, their punches and pinches were painful and persistent. One lucky shot to Sabrina's right eye left her momentarily dazed and blinded, but she managed to hold on to the giant leaf. With her free hand, she grabbed at the one

that looked like her and flung it off the vine. It fell silently past its comrades, who watched and shrieked. They began to retreat, but not before the one that looked like Uncle Jake stomped down hard on Daphne's fingers. She lost her grasp on the branch, and like the marionette, fell into the open blue sky and plummeted toward the ground.

4

efore Sabrina could scream, Puck let go of the beanstalk and dropped like a skydiver. Sabrina watched him, her heart pounding. She didn't breathe until she spotted his pink insect wings expanding and fluttering in the wind. He was too far away for her to see if he'd caught Daphne. She closed her eyes tight and prayed.

"Here's the piglet," Puck said. Sabrina opened her eyes to find him hovering in front of her. Daphne was wrapped around the boy fairy like a baby monkey, clearly terrified. Her complexion was slightly green and Puck struggled to free himself before Daphne's stomach rebooted itself. Sabrina snatched her away from him and held her like she might never let her go.

"You have to be more careful," Sabrina scolded.

"I will," Daphne whimpered.

Just then, an enormous boot came down and dug into the

beanstalk just above them. Its heel was smeared with the bodies of unfortunate animals and what looked like a few human skeletons. A horrible, rotting funk wafted into Sabrina's nose, but as much as she would have liked to pinch off the stink, she needed both hands to hang on to Daphne and the violently shaking beanstalk.

"I smell the blood of an Englishman!" the giant bellowed.

"No! You don't! We're from the Upper East Side of Manhattan!" Sabrina cried, scampering down the vine as fast as she could. "Puck, take Daphne again. Get her out of here."

Before Puck could help, the giant's big hand scooped the sisters up into its tight, sweaty grip and raised them so that they were eye to eye with his horrid, ruddy face. A tangle of overgrown hairs sprouted from his nose, and each of his broken teeth was a different shade of brown. A cloud of putrid air blasted out of his mouth that rivaled the smell of his boot.

"Don't worry. I've got everything under control," Puck said as he flew casually over to the giant's ear. He shouted something to the big brute that the girls could not hear. They were too busy screaming and praying. A moment later, Puck fluttered back down to them. "Allow me to introduce you to my assistant."

"What are you talking about?" Sabrina whimpered.

"I just recruited some help. Try to keep up, ugly," Puck said.

The giant reared its head and grunted at Puck.

"Not you!" Puck shouted, then pointed to Sabrina. "She's the ugly one."

The giant squinted at Sabrina and nodded.

"He's on our side," Puck continued.

"Friends!" the giant roared. Then, with a sudden jerk, the giant climbed down the rest of the beanstalk with ease. In no time at all, the children and their enormous sidekick were on the ground, though the giant still held them tightly ten feet off the ground.

The girls peered up at him suspiciously, unsure whether to trust Puck or kick their way down and run for their lives. Neither seemed a safe bet.

"He's really going to help us stop Pinocchio?" Sabrina asked.

Puck pointed across the farm. Pinocchio and his tiny helpers were bolting toward the forest not far away. "Hey, big guy, you see that boy running across the field?"

The giant grunted.

"That's the guy who stole your stuff. He's Jack."

The giant growled and took off across the farm, stomping on the little house beneath the beanstalk in his eagerness. Puck flew alongside his new recruit.

"You told him that Pinocchio is Jack?" Sabrina asked.

Puck nodded. "Better than telling him *you're* Jack."

Sabrina looked down at her clothes and saw she was wearing well-worn wool pants, a filthy shirt, and a cap. The Book had turned her into Jack.

"Good thinking," Daphne said. "You know, sometimes you're . . . you're Pucktastic!"

"New word?" Sabrina asked. Daphne had her own special vocabulary that seemed to materialize out of thin air.

Daphne nodded. "It means Puck-like in the best possible way."

Eventually, the giant stepped over Pinocchio to block his path. He spun around, set the girls down at his feet, and growled at the little boy.

"Step aside, brute," Pinocchio said.

"Fe! Fi! Fo! Fum!" the giant bellowed. "I smell the blood of an Englishman."

"You big idiot," the little boy said. "I'm not part of your story."

"Yes, he is," Puck shouted into the giant's ear. "He's Jack! Jack the Giant Killer. You know, in the killer of giants. Don't believe a word of what he says."

The giant roared and beat his chest like an overgrown gorilla.

Pinocchio stomped the ground in anger and stretched out his hand. In it he was holding a long black stick with a crystal star on the end. It crackled and popped with magical energy. He flicked it and a lightning bolt shot out and hit the giant in the chest. The giant cried out in rage and agony as he staggered back a step. Sabrina could see the attack had wounded him slightly, but his pride seemed to have taken a bigger blow. He looked perplexed that such a little boy could hurt him.

"Where did you get that?" Daphne asked Pinocchio.

"I've been seizing some unique items in the stories I've visited," Pinocchio said. "Some of them have proven to be quite useful. Take this fairy godmother's wand, which I acquired in the tale of Cinderella."

"It's going to take more than a sparkler to stop our friend here," Puck said, then turned to the giant. "Hey, big guy, are you going to let him get away? He stole the goose that lays the golden eggs!"

The giant roared again and leaped forward, only to be met with another painful shock. This one sent him down to one knee. He pulled himself back up to his feet, but Pinocchio was ready with another blast.

"We have to help," Daphne said. She scooped up a rock and rushed at the boy. Puck got out his wooden sword and followed. Sabrina clenched her fists and smiled. It had been a long time since she'd had a chance to use them, and she couldn't think of a better punching bag. While Pinocchio was distracted by the giant, the three children set on him, kicking and scratching. Puck smacked him in the mouth with his sword. Daphne kicked him in the shins. Sabrina punched and slapped. The combined assault forced the little boy to stop his attack on the giant and back away. When he could break free, he rushed into the woods and the children gave chase. They found him in a clearing where a magic door had materialized. Pinocchio opened it and turned to face his pursuers.

"It would be ill-advised for you miscreants to follow me," the boy said. "I have no qualms about hurting you."

"What did he say?" Puck asked.

"Who knows?" Daphne replied.

"Philistines!" Pinocchio cried, and then he stepped into the doorway and vanished. A moment later, the door disappeared as well.

"What does 'Philistines' mean?" Daphne asked.

Sabrina shrugged. "My best guess is he's calling us morons."

"I want to punch some of those big words right down his mouth," Puck said.

"I'm very worried you won't get your chance," Sabrina said. "Pinocchio just took our door. We may be stuck here."

"No problem," Daphne said as she removed the ball of magic yarn from her pocket. "We still have this." She leaned over and whispered something into the yarn, but it sat motionless in her hand. "It's not working."

"Because there isn't a door to find," Sabrina said. "It can't direct us someplace that doesn't exist."

"Oohg want to say thanks," the giant interrupted. "You make Oohg happy."

"Happy? How?" Daphne wanted to know.

"Oohg stomp through story many times. Each time Jack kill Oohg. This time, Oohg survive."

Sabrina frowned. "I'm afraid the Editor will come and fix that."

"Editor can try. Until then, Oohg going to enjoy new ending. Also, Oohg very honored to take part in celebration."

"Huh?"

"Meet my best man," Puck said, and then turned to the giant. "See you at the church, pal."

The giant nodded respectfully and ran into the woods. Trees were uprooted as they caught in his boots and were pulverized into mash. And then he was gone.

"Daphne miss Oohg," the little girl said. "Hmmm, Oohg Grimm . . ."

Sabrina rolled her eyes. "Mom would love that."

"I think she would! Oohg Grimm is Pucktastic."

"Hey, you think the Editor is sending revisers?" Puck asked.

Sabrina nodded. "I'm sure he is. Our new boss doesn't seem to have a problem erasing his employees."

They wandered into the woods until they found a pear tree. Puck shook it and dozens of plump, juicy treats fell around them. There was a clear pond only steps away, so the children washed the fruit and then sat under the tree for a feast. It was good to have something in their bellies. Sabrina, however, couldn't enjoy the snack because she was busy forcing down the panic rising in her throat. Her thoughts were haunted by images of little pink monsters pouring into the story and eating everything in sight. Without an escape door, there would be nowhere to run when the revisers came. All they could do was wait for the end.

"You two get some rest," Sabrina said. "I'll take the first watch."

Puck and Daphne didn't argue. They lay down and soon both were snoring. Sabrina looked down at them. When the revisers came, she wouldn't wake them. Better to die in their sleep, she thought.

To occupy herself, she found some smooth, flat stones by the pond and practiced skipping them along the surface of the water. She had seen people skipping stones on TV, but there was little opportunity to learn such a skill in Manhattan. Sure, she lived on an island bordered by a river and the ocean, but almost every square inch of land was paved.

Still, after some effort, she managed to get one to skip three times before it sank into oblivion. She searched the shore for more stones, collecting them in her pockets and in the belly of her shirt. When she'd had enough, she turned back to the pond only to see something unexpected rising from it. There was a creature in the water—no, better to say it was a creature made *from* the water. Though it was the shape of a man, it was made entirely of liquid. Leaves and pebbles swirled around in its body as it raced across the pond's surface toward her.

Sabrina was dumbfounded. Before she knew what was happening, its cold, wet hands were around her throat, squeezing tight. She fell back, spilling her stones at her feet and landing hard on the muddy ground. She tried to call out, but the creature's watery hands were so strong they cut off her ability to speak and breathe.

"Free me!" it bellowed. "Release me from this prison!"

Suddenly there was a blast of heat and the creature cried out. Momentarily stunned, its hands lost their shape and Sabrina took the opportunity to crawl out of its reach. When she turned to run, she saw Puck breathing fire at the water monster, causing it to boil and evaporate into steam. What was left of it sank back into the pond and disappeared.

"What was that thing, Grimm?" Puck asked as he helped her to her feet.

"I don't know for sure, but I have a theory that it was what everyone's been warning us about," Sabrina croaked. "The character from Snow White's story that was too horrible to keep. We're outside of Jack's story, in the woods. That's where this thing lives—in the parts of stories that aren't written. When it had me, it demanded that I set it free."

"What's going on?" Daphne asked as she rushed to the pond.

Puck shook his head. "Nothing."

Sabrina looked at him, silently thanking him for not causing the little girl any more worry.

"Well, come on. I have an idea on how to get out of this story," Daphne said.

Sabrina pulled herself together, and she and Puck followed Daphne back across the field in the direction they had come from.

"So, the Munchkins told us that the door appears when the story is over," Daphne said. "Well, the story is over, pretty much, and we're still here. Why hasn't it started over?"

"'Cause Jack didn't kill the giant," Sabrina reminded her.

"True!" Daphne said. "And now we have no Jack and no giant, but there is a big part of this story that is still around."

Daphne pointed at the enormous beanstalk rising into the clouds and continued her march to the little house beneath it.

Without knocking, Daphne opened what was left of the front door and went inside, returning after a second with a large ax. "It's just a theory, and I could be totally wrong, but maybe if we chop it down, the story will give us a break. Maybe if we can finish part of the story it will be enough of a finale to open a door."

Puck looked at the ax, then at the beanstalk. It was as thick and round as a house. "This smells suspiciously of work. You know I'm allergic."

"We have to try. Besides, there's nothing to eat in that house and so soon—"

"Give me that ax," Puck shouted, and snatched it from her hands. Soon he was chopping wildly at the enormous plant.

"It's worth a shot," Daphne said.

Sabrina nodded. Her throat was sore from the water creature's attack, and speaking hurt.

After each of them had taken their turns hacking at the beanstalk, the overgrown plant finally tottered over. Sadly, it fell on Jack's little house, crushing it even further. His poor mother would be distraught—she already had a loser for a son. But felling the beanstalk had its desired effect. A new door materialized right before them.

Sabrina pulled it open. A blast of wind blew everyone's hair back. It smelled like wild grass and tea. Daphne whispered for the ball of yarn to follow Pinocchio. It rolled into the void and the trio once again stepped into the unknown.

• • •

When the lights came back on, Sabrina found herself sitting at a long table set beneath a tree. A little cottage sat on a hill not far off and wildflowers covered the ground, leaning toward the sunlight. Sabrina looked around the table and nearly fell out of her chair when she saw who was sitting with her. The Mad Hatter was sipping tea from an enormous cup and resting his elbow on poor Daphne's head. Next to Daphne was a brown hare as big as a child, and he had his elbow on Daphne's head too. The little girl seemed just as bewildered by their arrival in the strange setting as Sabrina was. She also looked annoyed as she struggled to escape from the Mad Hatter and the hare's rude behavior.

Puck was at the other end of the table, shoveling handfuls of cake into his mouth. He looked like a boy who hadn't eaten in weeks. Not far away, Sabrina spotted the magic ball of yarn zipping into the woods.

Sabrina looked down at herself and saw she was wearing a soft blue dress with an apron tied around her waist. She also had on white stockings and simple black shoes and she knew exactly which story they had stumbled into.

"I'm Alice," Sabrina said through her strained throat.

"We're in Wonderland," Daphne squealed.

"Shhhhhhhh!" the Mad Hatter whispered. "Stick to the story."

"Have some wine," the hare said.

"Wine? Where do you think we are, France? I'm twelve years old," Sabrina said.

The hare seemed surprised by her outburst.

"Remember, you're supposed to be Alice," Daphne hissed.

"Well, Alice was only seven years old when this happened. They need to worry about getting arrested. You can't walk around offering alcohol to children."

"Do you know this story?" Daphne whispered.

Sabrina tried to recall what she knew of the story. For once, her memory didn't fail her—she knew the creature with the Mad Hatter was known as the March Hare. "I've read it a few times. It's so weird, so I needed to go over it again and again, especially during Mr. Canis's trial. I wanted to understand Judge Hatter."

The real Mad Hatter had been appointed by Mayor Heart so that he could intentionally rule against their friend in his murder trial. Despite the fact that the crime was eight hundred years old, and the girls managed to prove that someone else was responsible, the Hatter still sentenced Canis to death. Afterward, Canis had fled into the woods to hide.

"Your hair wants cutting," the Hatter said abruptly. Just like the real-life version, this Hatter had a huge head, and white hair as dry as hay and a tremendous hat. His face was filled with the now familiar nervousness of the characters they had encountered in the Book. He also shared the Book characters' bizarre, otherworldly appearance. The Mad Hatter looked almost like he was a walking illustration and not a real person. He seemed to have a thick outline around his entire body.

"Say something," Daphne whispered.

"I don't know what to say," Sabrina complained.

The Mad Hatter and the March Hare shared a worried look until the March Hare leaned over and whispered, "You should learn not to make personal remarks. It's very rude."

Sabrina sighed and repeated the phrase to the Mad Hatter.

"Why is a raven like a writing desk?" he said.

"Nuh-uh-uh," Sabrina said as she tried to get to her feet once more. "I'm not going to do the riddle part. I hate the riddle part. This goes on and on. Let's skip it."

"Skip it?" the Mad Hatter said as he forced her back into her chair. In the process he dropped his teacup. It shattered on the table.

"You fool!" the March Hare said, pointing his paw at the Mad Hatter. "That didn't happen. The Editor will be on us now."

"It was an accident. She made me do it!"

"The Editor won't care," the March Hare said. "What were you thinking? Going off the story! Well, I won't suffer for your lack of respect for the Editor. When his beasties arrive, I will tell them what you all have done. Why should I be revised? I'm innocent!"

"Throw me under the bus, will you!" the Mad Hatter shouted. He jumped to his feet and grabbed the March Hare by the neck. He shook him so angrily that the March Hare's bow tie unraveled. Enraged, the March Hare swung wildly and hit the Mad Hatter in the eye. The force from the blow caused him to fall backward over his chair. There he lay very still.

"Get up, you fool," the March Hare said. "When the Editor comes, it will do you well to show a little respect."

But the Mad Hatter didn't stir.

"Is he OK?" Daphne asked.

Sabrina circled the table and kneeled beside the Mad Hatter's body. She shook him gently. He was still breathing, but he was unconscious.

"You cold-cocked him," Puck said as he licked icing off his fingers. "Nice punch, too. For a rabbit."

The March Hare screamed in terror. "This is all your fault."

"Our fault? You're the one serving knuckle sandwiches," Daphne said.

"The Mad Hatter does not get beat up in the story!" the March Hare cried. He was panicking and pacing back and forth.

"Get control over yourself. We need to figure out what to do," Daphne said.

"Figure out what to do? This isn't spilled milk, child." The March Hare fled into the woods, knocking many of the teacups off the table as he went.

Watching him flee, Sabrina had an unsettling feeling that she, Daphne, and Puck should do the same. She grabbed them by the hands and they raced off into the woods, following the string that the ball of yarn had left.

"Shouldn't we wait for the Mad Hatter to wake up?" Daphne said.

"You remember what the Editor said," Sabrina responded. "His hungry little monsters show up and they eat. If we're in their way—we're lunch. We should go."

The little ball was fast and relentless. It was difficult for the kids to keep up. Everywhere they went they encountered bizarre people and talking animals, but the trio ran past them without a word. Sabrina would rather be accused of being rude than accidentally change *Alice's Adventures in Wonderland* any more than they already had. Eventually they found a small stream, and since they were too tired to go on, they stopped to take a break. The ball of yarn sat not far away, agitated and eager, like a soft, round bloodhound.

Puck lay down in the grass with his hands behind his head. "Ah, isn't this the life?"

Sabrina could hardly believe her ears. "What? You're enjoying this?"

"Aren't you? Jumping from one story to the next, playing around with history, changing people's destinies—this is first-rate mischief-making," Puck said.

"I will never understand you," she mumbled.

Puck laughed. "Really, don't you feel your heart beating! Don't you feel so alive? We've nearly died a dozen times already. It's exhilarating!"

Daphne laughed. "I'd lost count. Who can remember them all?"

"The last year of my life has been awesome. I hate to admit it, but you two have helped my street credibility in the prankster community. We've busted a guy out of jail, broken into someone's house, killed dragons and giants, destroyed a bank and an elementary school, changed the future, and started a civil war. You should be proud of yourselves."

Puck and Daphne laughed until they could hardly breathe. Sabrina, however, was horrified. She had been involved in all of those disasters and her choices had made them possible—sometimes even caused them directly. She jumped up and ran into the woods before anyone could see her tears.

She threw herself under a giant toadstool and wept until her body shook. She had never cried so hard or felt so lost.

"Let's get something clear," Puck said. His presence startled Sabrina, and she jumped to her feet. She felt awkward and exposed as she wiped the tears from her face, but Puck ignored her embarrassment. "I'm not going to hug you or let you cry on me. Don't get any funny ideas about that stuff. But, if you want to open your gob and spill your guts about your boo-boo face, feel free."

"I'm fine," she lied.

"You are smelly, annoying, infuriating, and I'm sure your parents dropped you on your head when you were a baby, but you are not fine. In fact, if I didn't know better, I would suspect a Levorian Ear Toad had burrowed into your brain. You haven't been yourself since we stepped into this book."

"Sorry to disappoint," Sabrina said as she stared off into the forest.

"Oh, boy!" Puck said. "Listen, I gave you a chance, but if you don't—"

"I'm scared," she said, hardly believing she had said it.

Puck grinned.

"Go ahead and laugh, dirtball, and I'll break your face," Sabrina said. She took a deep breath. She had a million fears: She was afraid of making bad decisions, getting her sister hurt, not finding her brother, failing. There was only one way to explain all of them. "I'm afraid of myself."

Puck arched an eyebrow. "Let's pretend I don't completely understand."

"I keep screwing up," Sabrina said. "In the last few weeks I've helped our greatest enemy destroy our house and kidnap our brother, and I raced into this crazy book without a second thought. Now we're working for this Editor, who might be evil, and his little pink erasers who might decide to eat us."

Puck rolled his eyes. "I suppose you want a pity party."

Sabrina's face flushed with anger. "So I open up to you and you make fun of me for it? You know what you are, Puck? You're a jerk."

Puck laughed as if Sabrina had just told him the funniest joke ever, which sent her into an even nastier rage. After all the time she had spent with this filthy boy she suddenly realized that he was exactly the same selfish, arrogant, and weird punk who had tried to push her into a pool not so long ago. How she could have ever considered him a friend, or even have feelings for him, was just more proof that she couldn't trust her own choices. She realized at that moment that if there was a decision she could be sure about, it was that she would never give this boy her heart. She didn't care what was supposed to happen in the future. "I'm going to find Daphne," she snapped, and stormed off, only to have Puck snatch her by the hand and roughly pull her to the ground.

"Are you crazy?" Sabrina said.

"Be quiet," he whispered, wrapping his hand around her mouth. "There are men coming. Lots of them."

Sabrina peered through the bushes and saw dozens of figures rushing through the forest. Each one had the body of a different playing card but with a head and arms and legs like a human.

Sabrina gasped. "Card soldiers!" She had encountered a few in the real world. Most worked for Mayor Heart and Sheriff Nottingham. They cared little for the rule of law unless it allowed them to cut someone in half with their swords.

"Where's Daphne?" Sabrina whispered.

Puck shrugged. "I left her by the brook."

Sabrina wanted to run to her sister, but all she could do was wait patiently for the strange army to pass.

Once they were gone, she and Puck crept out from behind their hiding spots and rushed to the stream. Daphne was nowhere to be found.

"Do you think they took her?" Sabrina asked. She felt as if she might faint.

"Hey," a voice said from above. Sabrina and Puck looked up and saw Daphne clinging to a tree limb high above their heads. "The card soldiers are everywhere. I can see hundreds of them. We should keep moving."

The children left as quickly as they could, but it soon became clear that something was following them. Something was jumping from one branch to the next, causing a shower of strange nuts to fall down on their heads. Puck, who had better eyesight than a non-Everafter, could not spot their stalker no matter how much he studied the trees. Even when he took to the air to search the branches, he couldn't see anything.

"Just keep moving," Sabrina said, doing her best to reassure Daphne. "It's probably a curious animal. When it gets bored, it will go find something else to do."

Unfortunately, all her attention on the strange stalker had distracted Sabrina from where they were going and who they were running from. They made a turn in the path only to stumble upon a crowd of card soldiers as menacing and vicious as any she had seen. Their leader, a very angry Nine of Diamonds, picked up the ball of yarn and then stepped forward with a sword aimed at Sabrina's heart.

"The Queen would like to make your acquaintance," the Nine of Diamonds said. Sabrina thought his invitation sounded a lot like a threat.

"Tell the Queen we're a little busy," Sabrina said.

The Nine of Diamonds scowled and stepped closer. "The Mad Hatter claims you told him you were from the real world. Her Majesty demands your presence."

"We don't know what you're talking about," Daphne lied.

"So, you aren't responsible for changing the story?"

The children looked at one another sheepishly. "Maybe a little."

"You are creating mayhem, and it is going to stop!" he shouted. The rest of his soldiers circled the trio and leveled their swords at their heads.

"I guess we can spare a few minutes for the Queen," Puck said. The children were marched through the forest until they came to a dirt road. There they saw several horse-drawn coaches racing along it—all of which were driven by frantic horsemen who looked as if their lives depended upon getting to their destinations as quickly as possible. "Out of the way!" They shouted at one another. "Royal business!"

The guards marched the girls into the heavy traffic, where they had to jump to avoid the speeding coaches and stay alive. The group pressed on until they came to a castle.

At the gate stood a guard with the head of a frog. He wore white leggings, a red coat with tails, and a white powdered wig like something out of an old romance novel, but his face was a muddy green and slick with slime. His big, bulbous eyes spun in their sockets yet he had a dignified, almost smug expression on his face.

"Are these the troublemakers?" the frogman croaked.

"Of course," the Nine of Diamonds said. "Let us pass."

The frog eyed them all carefully. "I don't know. You could be an impostor."

"Impostor? You know me! I was at your wedding," the soldier cried.

"One can never be too careful," the frog croaked.

"Well, I would think that the fact that I have a playing card for a body would be evidence enough of my identity."

"This conversation is too freaky," Daphne whispered to Sabrina.

The frog eyed the card soldier up and down and then let out a *harrumph*. "Keep a close eye on your prisoners," he warned.

The Nine of Diamonds scowled and pushed past the amphibious guard. He demanded the children follow closely and complained that they were pokey, as he led them into a damp and chilly tunnel beneath the castle. They emerged on the other side of the castle into a beautiful garden filled with exotic flowers in bright, vibrant colors and aromas. Several stone fountains sprayed crystalline water into the sky, creating shimmering rainbows. Everything was landscaped and manicured. The grass looked as if it had been trimmed by hand. Some of the details, however, were pure nonsense. As they stood beside the garden gate, Sabrina noticed a handful of card soldiers busily painting a bush's white rose bulbs bright red. When one of the soldiers splashed paint on another, they all broke into an argument that nearly turned into a fistfight.

"The Queen! The Queen!" someone shouted, and then a large procession of people entered the garden. There were trumpeters, court jesters, jugglers, mimes, and balladeers followed by ten card soldiers, followed by princes and courtiers decorated in diamonds, then ten children dressed in silk outfits decorated in hearts, then a group of very royal-looking men and women who appeared to be kings and queens, and finally a white rabbit in a little red smoking jacket who shooed everyone aside to allow for a soldier to enter carrying a velvet cushion with a crown on it.

"All eyes!" the rabbit chirped as he scanned the crowd with disdain. "The King and Queen of Hearts."

The Queen of Hearts and a rather sheepish-looking man with long hair and a beard entered to shrill trumpeting. Sabrina knew the Queen quite well. As the recently elected mayor of Ferryport Landing, she had nearly destroyed the town and taken an active interest in making the Grimm family's lives miserable. The King, however, Sabrina had never met. He looked just like the King of Hearts she had seen on packs of playing cards—complete with the strange beard that curled at the bottom. She had heard several conflicting stories about the King of Hearts. Some suggested he had decided to stay in Wonderland when Wilhelm Grimm offered to take everyone to America. Others claimed the Queen had murdered him in his sleep. Knowing the Queen of Hearts the way she did, Sabrina suspected that last rumor was true.

"Get to your places!" the Queen shouted as she charged through the crowd, knocking over soldiers and trumpeters as she went. "We're supposed to be playing croquet. We have to get this story back on track."

Everyone dashed off in a different direction only to return with a flock of gangly pink flamingoes and several squirmy hedgehogs. The Queen took one of the lanky birds and held it as if it were a croquet mallet. Then she placed the hedgehog on the ground and lined up the bird's beak with the hedgehog's behind. Then she swung wildly and missed her shot completely. Not that she could have hit the hedgehog. It wisely scurried off before the bird came down. The Queen chased after it, and with much aggravation and a dozen wild swings she managed only to knock the daylights out of seven attendants, one after another as they rushed in to help. Soon the playing field had a small but growing mountain of unconscious obstacles.

When she had spun herself in a half-dozen circles, she called for her attendants. "Where are the interlopers?!" the Queen railed.

The Nine of Diamonds pushed the children across the lawn until they stood before the dumpy and overheated Queen. "Your Majesty," the Nine of Diamonds said, "I have captured the three trespassers. They are responsible for the alterations to our important tale. I hope you are most pleased."

The Queen looked at the children and then turned to the

Nine of Diamonds and flashed him a disgusted expression. "Well, they can't very well play the game without mallets and balls."

"Of course," the Nine of Diamonds stammered, leaping into action. A moment later he returned with more flamingoes and hedgehogs. He shoved them into the children's hands. Sabrina's bird flapped furiously to free itself, showering her in pink feathers. Daphne's hedgehog hissed and bit at her before she set it on the ground where it promptly scurried away. Puck allowed his hedgehog to crawl up into his shirt.

"So you are from the real world?" the Queen said, swinging her flamingo at the furry ball. She missed again, but this time the force of the swing knocked her off her feet. Several of the soldiers helped her up and brushed her off with a great deal of energy until she slapped each of them in the head.

"Children, I am talking to you," she said.

Sabrina nodded. "Yes, we are not from this book."

"Interesting . . . ," the King of Hearts said.

The Queen flashed him an angry expression. "What would *you* know?"

He muttered an apology before lowering his eyes.

"It's your turn!" the Queen said to Puck.

Puck laughed. His flamingo had started a fight with Sabrina's bird and the two were producing a symphony of squawking and screeching. "I think I'm going to have to pass."

"Why have you come here?" the Queen asked.

Sabrina could barely look at her. Her fictional version was even more troubling and grotesque than the real Queen. Her head was gigantic and her arms and legs plump and short. It reminded Sabrina that this was not the real Mayor Heart. "We're searching for someone. A boy called Pinocchio. He's traveling with several wooden marionettes that can walk and talk."

"And pinch," Daphne said, showing the purple bruise on the back of her arm.

"Yes, he has been trespassing in our story as well. Bring the prisoner to me," the Queen said.

"You have him?"

"Yes, my guards arrested him earlier today," the Queen said. "He was creating a great deal of mischief."

"Since when is that a crime?" Puck asked.

As he ranted about his rights and freedoms to cause chaos and mayhem, Sabrina tried to process what the Queen had just told her. Did she really have Pinocchio in her custody? Could one of her family's bitterest enemies really be that helpful?

"The scamp has disturbed the flow of our story," the Queen said. "His presence has sent a ripple through everything—

changing dialogue, themes, and even characters. At this very moment I am supposed to be having an argument about beheading the Cheshire Cat, but as you can see, the cat is nowhere to be seen."

"I'm sure he's just running a bit late, Your Majesty," the White Rabbit said as he eyed a golden pocket watch fastened to a chain around his waist.

"Here comes the troublemaker," the King said, gesturing across the lawn.

Sabrina recognized the angry little boy at once. Pinocchio had a pointy nose, buckteeth, and little ears. He was wearing overalls and a red cap, and his hands were tied behind his back. Still, he struggled to get free from the guards, one of whom carried a birdcage in his hand. As they drew closer, Sabrina could see Pinocchio's marionettes were locked inside.

"You!" Pinocchio snarled as he glared at the children. "Why won't you let me be?"

"You betrayed us!" Sabrina said. "You think you can help Mirror kidnap a member of our family and we will just let it go? I thought you were some great intellect."

Daphne threw a punch into her open palm. "Let me at him."

"I didn't want to help the Master, but he was the only one who could provide me with this opportunity. When I asked the

Blue Fairy to make me into a real boy, I never imagined her magic would cruelly keep me this age forever. I was desperate for something everyone else takes for granted. I just want to become an adult and take advantage of my life."

"I've been this age for almost four thousand years," Puck said. "I kind of dig it."

"I suppose you're taking me back to the real world?" Pinocchio said.

Sabrina shook her head. "Not at all. We're turning you over to the Editor. What he plans to do with you, I don't know and I don't care."

Just then, four guards with axes on their shoulders approached. All wore black hoods that covered their faces, but their playing card bodies revealed them to be Aces from all four suits: diamonds, hearts, spades, and clubs. Behind them were more card soldiers, many of whom were carrying tree stumps on their shoulders.

"What's all this?" Daphne said, as the soldiers set up their tree stumps.

"Clearly we are going to execute this boy for crimes against our story," the Queen barked. "Off with his head!"

One of the hooded soldiers forced Pinocchio's head onto the stump while another sharpened his ax on a black stone.

"Whoa! Whoa! Whoa!" Sabrina cried. "You can't kill him!"

"We can't?" the King of Hearts said. "We have everything we need at our disposal to kill this criminal. Show her one of the axes."

The hooded guard flashed the deadly blade in Sabrina's eyes. "See, it's very sharp!" he said proudly.

"I'm not arguing that you *can* kill him," Sabrina exclaimed. "I'm saying that you shouldn't. The Editor wants him out of this story. He's caused enough problems and the more you change, the more has to be fixed."

The Queen let out a frustrated *harrumph*. "The Editor does what the Editor does. As the Queen of this Wonderland, my obligation is to pass judgment on every accused criminal here. Pinocchio entered our story with his marionettes and quickly went to work destroying it. That is a crime punishable by death."

"Don't let them kill me," Pinocchio pleaded as he fought against the much stronger men.

"The Editor can fix all this," Daphne said. "But if you kill the puppet, that's permanent."

"I'm not a puppet!" Pinocchio said.

"Dear, dear, I think I understand what the girl is saying," the King said, patting the Queen on the back. "The other children are jealous that they aren't being executed."

"Very well," the Queen said. "Consider it a gift from me to you. Off with their heads!"

"Keep your little butter knives to yourselves," Puck said. His sword was immediately in hand, but the card soldiers snatched him from behind, knocked his weapon to the ground, and tied his hands behind his back. Before Sabrina could react, the card soldiers had grabbed her and dragged her over to one of the stumps. Daphne was soon tied up as well, though she did manage to bite one of the guards on the hand.

"I'm sure you understand," the Queen said, "this is the only true deterrent to crime. In the hundreds of beheadings I have ordered, only a handful of the criminals have become repeat offenders."

"They were incorrigible, dear," the King said.

"On your command, Your Majesty," a hooded guard said.

Sabrina could not move. All she could do was look helplessly from the corner of her eye at the sharp ax above her.

The Queen cleared her throat. "Indeed. We can't very well be bothered by this inconvenience all day. We have a game of croquet to play. Good sirs! Prepare your axes!"

5

s the guard raised his ax, something fell out of the trees above and landed in the crowd with a grunt. Several of the soldiers were flung to the ground. Sabrina craned her neck to get a better look at the chaos and was surprised to find an enormous striped cat fighting the cards. It was nearly as big as she was, and had a bushy tail and a big mouth full of teeth. It swatted men left and right with its oversize paws, and despite its fierce assault, a clever, almost happy smile stretched across its face. His attack was accompanied by a high-pitched whistle, which signaled more bizarre creatures to rush into the melée. Soon a giant puppy and an odd bird with an enormous beak were fighting by the cat's side.

The card soldiers were befuddled. They jabbed their swords at the odd collection of animals. "Shoo! Shoo, you flea-bitten curses."

The animals held their ground. The puppy charged at the men and sent them flailing into the woods. The unusual bird slammed its hard beak into the heads of villains. From the Queen's party, the White Rabbit ran out to join them.

"What is the meaning of this?" the Queen bellowed.

"We're busting out!" the White Rabbit said, swinging his pocket watch threateningly. The Queen fell back in shock, and the rabbit turned his attention to the hooded guard. "If you know what's good for you . . ."

The guard set down his ax and ran, allowing the rabbit to untie Sabrina.

"Allow me to propose a deal," the creature said as it hopped over to untie Daphne. "In exchange for saving your lives, you will allow us to accompany you out of this book."

"What?"

"A simple business transaction, child. When you come upon the next door, you will allow my companions and me to join you with the intended goal of leaving the Book of Everafter. Do we have a deal?"

Sabrina was too distracted by the fighting to think clearly, but the little furry animal persisted.

"What say you?" the rabbit cried as it cut the bindings on Puck's hands.

The rabbit was so busy talking, he didn't notice a soldier rushing at him with a sword aimed at his chest. The giant cat leaped in the soldier's way, forcing him to stop in his tracks. He swung his weapon hard and fast at the feline's neck but just before it landed its deadly blow, the cat's body disappeared, leaving only his big, toothy grin behind.

"He's the Cheshire Cat," Daphne said, biting her palm.

The Cheshire Cat reappeared and grabbed the soldier's legs with its mouth. He dragged the distressed man up a tree to the highest branches and drove a sharp one right through its card body. It didn't seem to hurt the soldier, but it did leave him helpless, kicking and struggling to free himself. A moment later, the cat fell from the tree, only to land on all fours. He shook out his coat and smiled.

Meanwhile, the puppy took several of the villains in its mouth and wrenched them around violently before dropping them on the ground, dizzy and battered. The bird, whom Sabrina would later learn was a long-extinct dodo, knocked many of the men out with a swift clunk of its rock-hard head.

The White Rabbit mostly just barked commands and warned the others of approaching attacks. It wasn't long before the big animals had wiped out a majority of the Queen's army. Those who were still able fled into the woods, along with the Queen and the King and their flock of courtiers.

"Quick work," the dodo squawked.

"And not a scratch on us," the puppy said, before his attention turned to catching his own tail.

"Just as I predicted," the White Rabbit bragged. He stepped over some of the unconscious soldiers, bouncing on one's head before he reached the children. He bowed in respect. "Allow me to introduce myself."

"No need," Sabrina said, unable to hide her disgust. "We know who you are."

"I beg your pardon?"

"You're the White Rabbit and a member of the Scarlet Hand," Sabrina said.

"The Scarlet what?" the rabbit said.

"You're part of Mirror's army," Puck explained.

The rabbit turned to his friends and then reached up and felt his head. "Was I struck in the chaos? I'm having some trouble understanding this conversation. Children, I have never met any of you, ever. I'm sure I would remember. I don't know any 'Mirror,' nor have I ever counted myself amongst any army—certainly not a scarlet one."

"He's not lying," Daphne said, frowning. "We've never met him. This isn't our White Rabbit. This is the fake one from this stupid book."

Puck rolled his eyes. "All this real-world or storybook-world talk is giving me a headache. The only question that matters is: Can I roast him for dinner or not?"

"No," Sabrina said, finally understanding her sister's explanation. "Daphne's right. He's not a villain. None of them are."

"You come from the world outside the Book, correct?" the dodo said.

Sabrina nodded. "We're here looking for—hey! Where did Pinocchio go?" She scanned their surroundings. The little traitor was nowhere to be seen.

"He must have run off in all the chaos," Daphne said.

"This Pinocchio is important to you?" the dodo squawked.

"We're in this book to save our brother from a man known as Mirror. To stop him, we made a deal with the Editor. If we capture Pinocchio before he can make changes to his story, then the Editor will help us with our problem. We've been trying to find the little jerk and now we've lost him!"

"We can help," the Cheshire Cat said. "Then you can free us."

"Absolutely not!" Sabrina said. "You will slow us down."

"You agreed!" the White Rabbit argued.

"I did not," Sabrina said. "I barely understood a word you said. I was a bit distracted, trying to keep my head from being cut off."

"I'm not sure we can take them even if we wanted to," Daphne added. "They aren't real."

"The second we leave the Book, we'll be as real as you," the rabbit said.

"You don't want to leave this book anyway," Sabrina said. "The town we live in is on fire and our house is not much more than a demolition site."

"You say all that like it's a bad thing," Puck said, surprised.

"Anything would be better than the endless tedium of being a character in a story that never ends," the dodo said.

"What does 'tedium' mean?" Daphne asked.

"Tedium is kind of a boredom due to repetition."

"What does repetition mean?"

"Having to do something over and over again."

"It's like brushing your teeth or changing your underwear. Eventually you just give up," Puck said.

The Cheshire Cat ignored him. "This story never ends. When it gets to the last page, we are all sent back to the beginning. Each day we say the same things, wear the same clothes, and a few of us meet the same untimely deaths. Imagine living a life where you cannot make your own decisions lest you be devoured and rewritten. Imagine being stuck in the same day, forever and ever."

"I just want to chase squirrels!" the puppy whimpered. "That's all, but the Editor is mean. I did it once and he sent the monsters to fix me."

"None of us volunteered to be in a living history book, and no one asks us if we are happy. The Editor is unsympathetic to our plight; thus, we have come to this drastic decision. The only way to escape our bondage is to escape the Book," the White Rabbit said.

"The Editor is not going to be happy," Sabrina warned. "We've met him, and he doesn't seem like the kind of guy who's going to be pleased that you four are taking a vacation."

"Who put him in charge? He rules over us without thought or mercy," the dodo said. "Any little change in the story and our very existence is wiped clean."

"If things are so bad, why haven't you gone through one of the doors yourself?" Daphne asked.

"We've tried!" the puppy barked. "We can't open the doors. Only outsiders can do that."

Sabrina took a deep breath. She wished she could get away and think. That was the problem with being a Grimm—there was never any time to contemplate a decision. If only she could find a quiet tree and some time to analyze the characters' requests. She hadn't been lying about the Editor; she suspected he would be furious. But she could also be sympathetic. When she found out he was the Master, Mirror had told her a little of what his life was like as a prisoner. She would have done anything to free him if she'd known he was suffering, but he had never shared his pain. These four characters, strange as they were, wanted something she might be able to provide. On the other hand, they were four more people who were going to turn to her to lead them. They were four more people putting their lives and destinies in her hands. No! They couldn't come. What if something went wrong?

"All right, you can come with us, but let's get something clear, first," Daphne said before Sabrina could answer. "We're not strolling through these stories because they're fun. We're looking for Pinocchio. We can't have anyone slowing us down. You fall behind—you're on your own. If you get hurt, we will leave you. If the Editor sends revisers after you, we cannot stop to save you, and trust me, they're gross—so keep up!"

"Agreed," the White Rabbit said. "We will not be a burden. And in return, we offer our assistance in your search. This Pinocchio you speak of sounds like a powerful foe. You may need all the help you can get."

"I will bite him!" the puppy said.

"Leave the biting to the experts," Puck said, and bared his teeth.

"There's just one last thing," Sabrina said as she searched the ground for the unconscious body of the Nine of Diamonds. When she found him, she leaned over and snatched the ball of magic yarn out of his pocket. The old tingle of magic was there so she quickly tossed it to Daphne. The Cheshire Cat let out a loud squeal and leaped into the air. He caught the ball in his mouth and landed on all fours. Then he spit it out and batted it back and forth with his striped paws.

Daphne shrieked and rushed over and yanked it from his grasp. "Bad kitty," she chastised. "This is our way out of here. It's leading us to Pinocchio."

"Intriguing," the White Rabbit replied. "I don't mean to be rude, but I believe it would be wise to get out of this particular story as soon as possible. The Editor has to have noticed the changes to our story by now."

"I agree!" the dodo cried.

"Luckily, we're at the end of this tale, so all we have to do is find the door," Daphne said, and then whispered instructions to the yarn. It hopped out of her hands and rolled into the woods. They gave chase and soon came to a door standing amongst the bank of trees. As she was the first one to arrive, Daphne turned the doorknob, and it swung open with a blast of wind so powerful Sabrina feared it might knock her off her feet.

Struggling against the violent air, she turned and urged her new companions to follow. "This is it!"

"Be brave, friends," the White Rabbit said to his fellow rebels. He smoothed out the wrinkles in his jacket and slid a monocle in front of his eye. Then he hopped forward and disappeared through the doorway. The puppy let out a happy howl and rushed in after him. The Cheshire Cat tucked his head down and pulled his ears back, and a moment later he was gone too.

"I had my doubts this day would come," the dodo said as he stared at the open doorway.

"Save it for your diary, pal," Puck said, kicking him in the behind and forcing him into the abyss. "We're in a hurry."

A moment later, the children were charging forward into the unknown. When the world came back into focus, the group found themselves in the thick undergrowth of a huge forest. Almost immediately they spotted Pinocchio several yards from where they were standing. The boy was bent over, with hands on his knees, trying to catch his breath. When he spotted them, he cursed creation itself and then hefted the birdcage he had taken from the card soldiers and freed his wooden minions.

"Keep these fools away from me," Pinocchio ordered. Then he dashed off into the forest.

"Not the puppets again!" Sabrina complained.

"Don't worry, honey bunny," Puck said as the creatures raced toward them. "I won't let anyone put a finger on my sweet-ums."

The Trickster King never got a chance to defend her—or himself. The marionettes hopped onto his back and legs. They untied his shoelaces and yanked on his hair. When he managed to brush them off, they jumped onto Sabrina. She swatted at them, but even when she managed to knock one off, another took its place.

Finally, the dodo helped out—first it smashed the marionette that looked like Granny Relda, and then the one made to resemble Veronica, Sabrina and Daphne's mother, with its hard head. That left only the figures that looked like Daphne, Uncle Jake, and Henry Grimm, father of the Grimm girls. The Cheshire Cat snatched them up in his mouth while the puppy furiously dug a hole. The cat spit them out and the dog buried them. All of the marionettes had finally met their end.

Sabrina charged into the woods after Pinocchio, and after only a few steps she spotted him. He was standing before a giant shoe. It was nearly twenty feet high and was brown with a gigantic and tarnished brass buckle on top. Carved into the shoe's heel was a door decorated with a festive garland and a little mat on the ground that read WELCOME. Sabrina watched the boy swing the door open, rush inside, and slam the door behind him.

"No way!" Daphne said as she caught up with Sabrina.

"What?" the Cheshire Cat asked when he and his friends joined the children.

"This can't be real," Sabrina said.

"Hello?" Puck cried impatiently. "What story is this?"

"It's 'The Little Old Lady Who Lived in a Shoe,'" Daphne said, and then bit into her palm.

"Never heard of it," the dodo squawked.

"Never heard of it?" Daphne exclaimed. "Everyone knows this story."

"I don't," Puck said. "If it's in a book, I'm blissfully unaware of its existence."

"It goes like this, 'There once was an old lady who lived in a shoe; she had so many children she didn't know what to do.' Honestly, I don't know the rest."

"There's no monster?" Puck said.

Daphne shook her head.

"No dragon? No witch? No one gets eaten?"

"No," Sabrina said.

"Then what are we doing out here? Let's go in there and grab that pointy-nosed loser," Puck said. He marched up to the door and threw it open, only to be drowned in a flood of filthy children squeezing out of the door and running into the woods. There were hundreds, maybe even thousands. It was hard to tell, as they just kept coming and coming like the bubbles in a shaken bottle of soda. The dodo snatched the puppy and flew into the air while the rabbit straddled the cat and was carried high into the branches of a tree. Sabrina and Daphne had to leap out of the way to avoid being trampled.

A frail old woman appeared in the doorway. "Have fun!" she called. "And don't be late for supper. We're having broth."

She spotted the group of interlopers, eyed them angrily, and whispered, "Go away," before slamming the door closed.

The girls rushed to help Puck to his feet. The poor boy had been trampled and had little shoe prints all over his body.

"Are you OK?" Sabrina said.

"I would have preferred a monster," Puck said, much the worse for wear.

"He's using the children to escape," Daphne said. "He's hiding in the crowd."

"I'll get him!" Puck said as his wings sprang from his back. They flapped a bit, but he didn't seem to have the energy to get off the ground.

It was pointless anyway. A door appeared across the clearing and Pinocchio raced toward it from the woods. Before anyone could stop him, he had slipped through and slammed it behind him. The door then dissolved before their eyes.

Sabrina sat down beside the shoe. She was tired, hungry, and angry. She knew everyone was looking to her for answers. But besides her sister and Puck, she couldn't have cared less about any of them.

"I beg your forgiveness, but what do we do next?" the White Rabbit asked. "Shouldn't we go after the boy?"

"We eat," Puck said. Sabrina wondered if the boy's sudden leadership was his way of taking some of the pressure off of her, but then she shook her head. Puck was incapable of being so sensitive.

The rabbit and the cat groused a bit but said nothing that would start an argument. The puppy sniffed the air and claimed he could lead them to wild berries. Sabrina wasn't sure it was wise to step outside the boundaries of the story again. The last thing she or the others needed was another encounter with that . . . that *thing* that lurked there. Still, everyone was famished. There was no point in putting everyone in danger, so she insisted that Puck and Daphne and the others stay behind.

She and the puppy searched for the fruit and came across a bank of walnut trees and an abandoned garden filled with carrots and cucumbers. Sabrina filled her pockets with all she could carry and headed back to the camp. While they were gone, Puck had built a fire. It was far bigger than they would need, but once they got it under control they sat and shared the food with the others.

"Please tell us of the real world," the Cheshire Cat begged as he munched on some berries.

"Yes," the puppy dog yipped. "What's it like?"

"Well, that depends on who you ask," Sabrina said. "Most people live pretty uneventful lives."

"But not you?" the White Rabbit said.

Puck laughed. "Not at all."

"Yeah, our lives are nonstop excitement," Daphne said. "We're always fighting monsters and saving the world."

"Monsters!" the White Rabbit cried.

"Just in our hometown," Sabrina said. "The rest of the world, for the most part, is happily dull. Unfortunately, once you step into Ferryport Landing, you'll be as stuck there as you are in this book. There's a spell that traps Everafters within the town limits."

The animals shared uncomfortable looks and were quiet for a moment.

"I'll happily trade this prison for another," the dodo said. "At least there is no one watching your every move and making sure you do as you're told."

"You mentioned that I was different from your White Rabbit," the rabbit said sheepishly.

"Yeah, he's a jerk," Puck said, his face smeared with purple juice. "Evil, too. Not that being evil necessarily makes you a bad person or anything."

The White Rabbit gasped. It was easy to see he was offended.

"See, the real White Rabbit is a member of a very mean group called the Scarlet Hand. They're trying to take over the world," Daphne explained.

"This boy you're chasing, Pinocchio . . . Is he their leader?" the Cat asked.

"No, but he's a member," Sabrina said. "Their leader is traveling through this book too. His name is Mirror. He's the magic mirror from Snow White's story. He was a friend of ours, or at least we thought he was. But he betrayed us and kidnapped our little brother. He wants to steal his body for himself so that he can be a real person."

"Well, you have my help, and if I can speak for the others, all of our help," the dodo said.

The puppy dog growled. "It is the very least we can do for the amazing opportunity you are giving us."

The characters continued their questions about the world of the living. They were fascinated with little things like cars and phones and indoor plumbing. The White Rabbit had a difficult time accepting the idea that the real world had very few talking animals.

"It's got very few clinically insane hat-makers too," Sabrina grumbled.

Eventually, the berries and nuts were gone and all the chatter started to give Sabrina a sharp headache. She told Puck to shout for her if a door appeared and then excused herself to walk into the woods for some solitude. She knew she'd hardly be missed. The refugees from Wonderland continued their party with songs and stories of the lives they intended to build in the real world. They were prisoners broken from their cages, and it was a day to rejoice, but Sabrina didn't feel much like celebrating.

"Mind if I sit?" Daphne asked, appearing from nowhere.

"Where's Puck?"

"He's got the puppy chasing his own tail and he's laughing like an idiot," the little girl said as she sat down against a tree. "I've come to ask you what you've done with my sister."

Sabrina shook her head. "I don't understand."

"I know you aren't really Sabrina Grimm," Daphne said. "I

know you are a fake. The real Sabrina doesn't act like you at all. For instance, my sister never asks other people for their opinions on what she should do."

Sabrina sighed.

"Normally, I find it annoying," Daphne continued. "I mean, she almost never asks me what I think, and that makes me fighting mad sometimes. But never, in all the time we've spent in Ferryport Landing, has she ever, ever, ever, ever, ever asked Puck what to do. Who are you, and what have you done with the real Sabrina Grimm?"

"I'm afraid I'll make the wrong choices."

Daphne was quiet. "'Cause you trusted Mirror and he turned out to be the bad guy?"

Sabrina was surprised by her sister's insight. It was another sign that Daphne wasn't such a little girl anymore. "How did you guess?"

"Uh, I trusted him too," Daphne said. "He was like an uncle to me. When he turned out to be the Master, I couldn't believe I hadn't figured it out myself. I looked back on all our time with him and I started to see the clues: the two faces he showed—one for the reflection and one for the Hall of Wonders, and the fact that whenever we were discussing a plan around him the bad guys always seemed to know, and all those mirrors we found around town—Nottingham and Heart have a couple, and Oz had one in his workroom. There was one in Rumpelstiltskin's office. I'm sure Jack had one in his apartment. He was sending messages to his evil army through them. Why didn't I see it? I'm a Grimm. I'm a detective. I have mad fighting skills and can zap someone with a magic wand like nobody's business . . . but I didn't see it."

"If you made the same bad decision to have trusted him, why aren't you panicking now?" Sabrina asked.

Daphne shrugged. "Mirror wants us to be off balance. That way we'll have a tougher time stopping him. I'm not going to let him keep messing with me."

"But when the people in your life betray you, how do you know which decisions are right?"

"Who knows what the right thing is anymore?" Daphne said as she munched on the last of her walnuts.

"What do you mean?"

"Well, I've been thinking about what Mirror is doing. He's clearly lost his mind, and it's horrible what he's trying to do, but you know, he kind of has a point. He's been trapped in that mirror for hundreds of years. He's had owners who were cruel to him. He wants out, so he can be like the rest of us. He's still a monster, but I can see where he's coming from.

"And this Editor, well, his job is to keep the stories the same. If he doesn't, then it affects the real world. The Editor has to fix this stuff, which isn't fair to the characters, but it's his job.

"And then there's the people in this book. Why should they have to sit in some boring story all the time? That's not fair."

"You're quite the sympathizer," Sabrina said.

"Pretend I'm not a dictionary and I don't know what that word means."

"It means that you understand the problems of others," Sabrina said.

"I guess I do, but not when you mess with my family. Whether Mirror has a point or not, he hurt me and you and everyone I love. That's when I know when my decisions are right or wrong. Protecting my family will always be right."

Sabrina blinked. "And you're accusing *me* of being an impostor. When did you get so wise?"

"Back at home, Puck and I have been staying up and watching old westerns on TV," Daphne said. "All the cowboys talk like that."

• • •

When Sabrina and Daphne returned to the group, the fire had died down and the others were waiting expectantly.

"What now?" the Cheshire Cat asked.

Sabrina turned to Daphne. The little girl gave her a knowing look and then smiled. It was a relief to have her sister's approval.

"I think we need to re-create the ending. This story is so short it might be easy. New ending—new door."

"Interesting. But how?" the White Rabbit said.

"This little old lady lives in a shoe. She's got so many kids she doesn't know what to do. Sounds like she needs a little help organizing," Sabrina said. "Puck, can you take the others and find the children? Get them back to the shoe on the double. Daphne and I will stay here and get everything ready."

It wasn't long before the children were hurrying back to the house. It helped that Puck had transformed himself into a pterodactyl and was buzzing over the crowd so that they ran for their lives. When the children were gathered, Sabrina looked out on the hundreds of them.

"All right, kids, listen up," Sabrina said. "You have had it too easy. Your mother feeds you, clothes you, washes your laundry, and keeps your rooms clean. She's exhausted. She's inside taking a much-needed nap. While she's having a little 'me' time, we're going to get this shoe in shape. So, if your name starts with the letter 'A,' raise your hand."

A dozen children raised their hands.

"You are going to mow this yard, rake the leaves, and clean out the gutters," Daphne said.

The children whined.

"No fuss!" Sabrina cried. "If your name starts with 'B,' you're on laundry. There's a pile of dirty socks in there a mountain high. They need to be washed, dried, folded, and put away."

"If your name starts with a 'C,' you've got dish duty," Daphne added. "Wash, dry, and put away. And remember, there is a trick to loading the dishwasher. Don't overfill it!"

The chores went on all the way to Zed, Zelma, and the rest of the Zs. Sabrina and her group stood by and watched as the children washed windows, swept the walkway, bagged grass clippings, and beat the dust out of rugs. When the little old woman came outside, she had tears in her eyes.

"Thank you! Thank you!" she cried.

Just then, a door appeared behind Sabrina. "Let's get the ball rolling," she said to her sister.

Daphne whispered something into the magic yarn and it hopped out of her hand. When Puck opened the door, it rolled right through it. Puck was next, followed by Daphne. Sabrina gestured for the others to follow and stepped through the portal last, unsure of where they would land.

• • •

When Sabrina could see again, she was at the bottom of a rocky hill crowned with a majestic castle. It overlooked a crisp green valley and a churning river less than a mile away. Unlike the crumbling castles Sabrina had seen in her father's travel magazines, this one was pristine—almost as if it were brand-new. Its walls were constructed from gleaming white stones and its towers stretched toward the clouds. A turret sat on the rooftop, where a proud orange flag featuring a fierce black griffin flapped in the wind. Before Sabrina could ask her sister which story they had entered, there was a loud explosion and the blue sky turned an angry red.

"Dear, dear," the Cheshire Cat said as it hid behind Daphne. "We've stepped into a war zone."

There was another explosion that echoed across the valley, and a moment later, one of the castle's towers toppled over and crashed against the rocks below. The next thing Sabrina knew, three knights in full armor came charging over a drawbridge and straight toward them. Sabrina stepped out of the way only to fall to the ground with a thud. She wasn't expecting to be wearing a heavy suit of armor.

Puck pulled her to her feet with much effort.

"Sir Galahad! Sir Bedivere!" one of the men in armor shouted to the girls. It was suddenly clear they had been placed in the roles of knights. "The Editor has sent a sorcerer to put down our rebellion. He has invaded the castle and our dear Merlin is fighting him off, but he is very powerful. He has attacked the castle, but he will not stop our cause. Freedom will be ours."

"Cause?" Sabrina asked. "What cause?"

"To escape this book, of course," the second knight said proudly. "We are members of the Character Liberation Army. We are working to leave this story, and clearly the Editor has unleashed a horror on us aimed at ending our quest."

The third knight looked as if he were ready to add more to the conversation when he rubbed his eyes and stared at the group. "What manner of creatures are you?"

Sabrina turned to look at her group—a giant puppy, an extinct bird, a rabbit wearing clothes, a man-size cat, a boy with pink fairy wings . . . not to mention Daphne and herself, two little girls in ill-fitting suits of armor.

"Long story," Sabrina said to the knight. "What story is this?"

The third knight gasped. "You've come from another story?"

"Can it be?" the first knight cried.

"You are in league with the Editor!" the second knight shouted. At once, the three knights removed their swords from their sheaths.

Puck pulled out his own toy sword. "All right, people. Don't do something you'll regret."

Sabrina raised her hands to calm everyone down. "We're not here to stop you. We're chasing someone—a little boy."

"If the villain fighting Merlin inside is a little boy, the world is certainly doomed," the third knight said.

There was another eardrum-rumbling explosion, and part of the castle's walls crumbled into dust.

"This sorcerer . . . Can you take us to him?" Sabrina asked.

"Take you back into the castle?" the third knight cried. "Are you daft?"

"If you won't take us, we'll go on our own." Daphne took slow, deliberate steps forward in her armor. It wasn't long before she tipped over face-first. "Stupid suit of armor! Whose idea was it to wear two hundred pounds of metal into battle? A duckling could kill me right now."

Sabrina and Puck helped the little girl to her feet. Once she was up, the other knights dismounted and helped them remove some of the heavier pieces of armor. When the first knight, who introduced himself as Sir Port, removed Sabrina's helmet, he nearly took her nose with it. Soon, the girls were moving about a bit more freely.

"You're fools," Sir Port said. "But we'll take you back to the castle."

The dodo cleared his throat. "Perhaps we should wait here until all the fighting is over."

"Remember the deal, bird," Sabrina chirped. "We won't come back for you."

"I must object," the rabbit interjected as he polished his monocle. "The two of you have taken on roles in this story. We have a freedom you do not. Any number of horrible things could happen to you. Perhaps it would be wise to entrust your yarn to us. Just in case."

Sabrina eyed the group suspiciously. "The yarn is ours, buster."

The White Rabbit threw up his paws. "Of course! Of course! Just a suggestion."

Despite their vocal complaints, Sabrina didn't turn back to see if the characters were following. She, Puck, Daphne, and the three knights on horseback climbed up the steep hill and crossed a wide wooden drawbridge over a black and foul-smelling moat.

Through a great arch they could see a smoke-filled castle courtyard. As they entered, Sabrina spotted a crowd of panicked knights, ladies-in-waiting, and court jesters rushing about willy-nilly trying to avoid a terrific battle. The fighting seemed to be coming from the center of the courtyard. Sabrina could feel the familiar tingle of enchantments all around her, though the sonic booms and flashes of white-hot light were all the evidence she needed to determine that someone was wielding some very powerful magic.

They pushed their way through the crowd and eventually found a space with a view of the conflict. The power of the attacks was so intense that Sabrina had to shield her eyes, but inside the fire and light she could make out two figures. They circled each other with hands afire and eyes burning with raw power. The air crackled with energy every time one of them made the slightest movement.

"What's happening?" Daphne asked a tall, handsome man with flowing black hair.

When Sabrina looked up into his face, she immediately recognized him as Sir Lancelot, one of Ferryport Landing's dashing volunteer firefighters. Granny Relda had recently purchased a "Firefighters of Ferryport Landing" calendar, and when she took a peek at it when it arrived in the mail, her face turned as red as a stoplight. Sabrina never saw the calendar again and the old woman wouldn't say where it had gone.

With his familiar face, she could place the story: They had

stepped into the tale of King Arthur and his Knights of the Round Table.

"This cursed interloper hath stepped through an enchanted doorway in the midst of our castle," Lancelot said. "A battalion of noble knights and I naturally came to the defense of Camelot, but we were soon overwhelmed by the villain's magics. The king's adviser, Merlin, was called, and due to his experience with the black arts, has unleashed his ungodly powers on the Editor's lackey."

"What did he say?" Daphne asked.

Sabrina shrugged. She had trouble understanding his real-life counterpart back home.

"Pinocchio sure has learned the ins and outs of that magic wand," Daphne said as they watched the fighting. "That's powerful magic for a little boy."

"Little boy?" Lancelot said. "The boy is not fighting Merlin. It's his father who is creating such chaos."

Sabrina strained to look into the battle once more. She could make out Merlin, old and feeble, fighting off a short, thin, balding man in a black suit.

"It's Mirror!" she cried.

"If he's fighting, where is Rodney?" Daphne said.

"Rodney?"

"Fine!" Daphne said. "Where's what's-his-name?"

"If it's the child you speak of, he is there, with the queen," Lancelot said as he pointed across the courtyard to a slender, pale woman with blond hair that hung to her hips. She wore an eggshell-white silk dress and her hair was embellished with tiny, delicate flowers. In her arms was a small boy with red hair and bright green eyes.

The children shoved and forced their way through the crowd as they hurried to their brother. Most people were too distracted by the fighting to care they had been pushed, but they were also too distracted to move out of the way. Still, Sabrina pressed on and soon she, Daphne, and Puck were standing before the lovely woman and the baby boy.

"Guinevere!" Sabrina said. She had met the woman a few times when her grandmother went on errands and always found her to be sweet and polite. She was a stark contrast from her hot-headed husband, Arthur.

"Do I know you, child?"

"The real you does," Sabrina said.

"We're from outside the story," Daphne said.

Guinevere's eyes grew wide. "Then word of our efforts has reached far and wide. Have you come to help liberate us?"

"Not exactly. The little boy you're holding is real too. He's our brother," Sabrina said.

Guinevere pointed to Mirror. Lightning bolts were coming out of his hands and eyes. "He told me to guard him with my life," the queen said. "I fear he means it."

"He belongs with us," Sabrina said as she took the boy into her arms. She looked into his face. She had never been so close to him, and only days ago she had no idea he existed, but now, looking into his eyes, smelling his skin, feeling his little fingers wrap around her neck, she could feel he was family. This strange boy was as familiar to her as her own sister. He was as much a part of her as her own hands.

"We have to get out of here while Mirror is distracted," Daphne said.

"Plus, that kid needs a diaper change," Puck added.

"I think that's you," Sabrina said. "But you're right."

"What about Pinocchio?" Daphne said. "We made a deal with the Editor."

Sabrina scanned the crowd, but there was no sign of the boy. "I know a deal's a deal, Daphne, but we're in way over our heads. Let's take our brother and get out of here while we still can. Tell the ball of yarn to take us home."

For once, Daphne did not argue. She whispered her instructions into the ball, but it sat in her hand.

"We're not at the end of this story," she said. "The last thing that happens is a wounded Arthur is put in a boat with fairies and they drift down a river. With things all messed up like this, I can't even begin to imagine where we might be in this story right now."

"Editor! Open the door!" Puck shouted over the noise.

"What are you doing?" Sabrina said.

"The Editor said to call for him when we were ready," Puck said. "Editor! Where are you?"

"But we don't have Pinocchio yet," Sabrina said.

"A tiny detail when you consider we're about to be killed," the boy fairy shouted.

Suddenly, the ball of yarn rolled out of Daphne's hand and darted into the crowd. The children gave chase and struggled against the relentless tide of onlookers. Each step was a challenge as they were jostled and shoved mercilessly. But Sabrina couldn't have cared less. Her heart was full with joy. The child in her arms completed her family, and the hole inside her could start to mend itself. Daphne ran alongside with happy tears in her eyes. Even Puck, who despised the joy of others, had a tight grin on his face. For once, the Scarlet Hand had not succeeded.

And then there was an explosion that knocked them off their

feet. Sabrina checked to see if her brother was hurt, but besides a few startled cries he was in perfect health. Puck helped her to her feet but there was an eerie quiet in the courtyard and then a troubled murmuring.

"He killed Merlin," a voice said near them. "I can't believe it. He actually killed him."

Then a familiar voice bellowed a demand that seemed to hover over the crowd like an angry cloud. "WHERE IS THE BOY?"

"Daddy!" the child cried.

The children looked at the toddler in shock.

"Daddy?" Daphne repeated. "Mirror isn't your daddy."

Her argument was cut short as an invisible wave raced through the crowd and forced a path from the center of the battle to the children. As the path cleared, Sabrina could see Merlin lying on his back, his empty eyes focused on the blue skies above. Standing over him was Mirror. Sabrina had seen his face full of rage before, but that was only when he appeared in the magic mirror. She had never seen the kind, soft face that she saw when she stepped inside the Hall of Wonders the slightest bit angry. She quaked with fear.

Daphne seemed just as terrified. Puck, however, stepped

forward. For once his bravado and boasting were gone. She had seen him fight giants, dragons, and Jabberwockies with a gleam in his eye and a grin on his face; this time he was deadly serious.

"It's over, Mirror," he said.

With a flip of his hand, Mirror tossed aside hundreds of people in the courtyard. Then he strolled forward with a smile on his face.

"So the boy fairy comes to the rescue once more," Mirror said. "When we first met, I would never have thought you to be the hero. But look at you—your hand is on your sword. Your face is hard. You're like a smelly James Dean—a rebel without a clue."

Puck said nothing.

"You've thrown your lot in with the Grimms. Not a bad decision. They're good people," Mirror continued. "If a little simple. Still, they would have treated you right."

"'Would have'?" Puck said.

"Oh, yes, but you wouldn't give me the child, and I was forced to kill you," Mirror said.

Puck smiled. "You're welcome to try, you sorry excuse for a reflection, but I think you'll find the Trickster King more than formidable. If I were you, I'd walk out of this story before I break you into a million tiny pieces of glass."

"As stubborn as you are pungent," Mirror said as he raised his hands. Sparks flickered out of his fingers, and his eyes glowed with power. "I'm afraid you are going to make one very smelly corpse."

6

irror's hand burst with light. Long tendrils of energy exploded out of his fingertips and crashed into Puck's chest. The boy's sword fell from his hand and he was shot backward several yards.

"Stop it!" Sabrina demanded.

Puck slowly stood up and a weak smile came to his face. "Your joy buzzer doesn't hurt that much."

Mirror shook his head and shocked Puck again, with similar results. "The three of you are becoming tiresome. I know you are upset with what I did, but as the saying goes, 'desperate times call for desperate measures.' I've been trapped in the Hall of Wonders for hundreds of years as the slave of others, including your family. I had nearly given up hope of ever having my freedom, but I saw an opportunity and I took it. If you had been locked in a prison with no hope of ever being free, you would do drastic things in order to escape too."

Sabrina rushed to Puck's side. "I wouldn't kidnap someone's parents and force their children into an orphanage. I wouldn't steal an innocent child from his family and involve him in a twisted plan to take his body."

She tried to keep Puck lying down, but he stood again. "Is that all you got?"

Mirror ignored him. "Starfish, my deception gave me no joy. If I could have taken another child, I would have, but your family is the only human family I've had contact with in decades. When I heard that your mother was pregnant, I knew I had to act."

"So we were easy prey?" Daphne asked.

Mirror frowned and lowered his hands. The power in them faded and his anger seemed to go with it. "You can't understand, and I don't have time to argue about it. The Editor is probably preparing to revise this story as we speak."

Just then, there was a horrible scream from behind Sabrina. She turned to find a mob of people rushing in her direction.

"They're coming!" someone cried. "Run for your lives!"

The crowd stampeded through the courtyard while a few desperate knights struggled to raise the drawbridge. King Arthur passed by Sabrina in the crowd, his magical sword Excalibur raised and ready.

"What's going on?" Sabrina said, keeping one eye on Mirror.

"The Editor hath sent his filthy creatures upon us," he said.

"Revisers!" Mirror said. For the first time in her life, Sabrina could see fear in the little man's face.

There was a terrible crunch, and when Sabrina turned around she saw that the drawbridge had come crashing down. A wave of pink revisers scurried on tiny limbs into the courtyard. Arthur and his knights raced to fight them back, slashing desperately with their swords. Mirror disappeared in the bustle.

"If any of you want out of this story, follow us," Sabrina shouted. With her brother in her arms, along with Daphne and Duck and their companions from Wonderland, she followed the yarn as it weaved a haphazard path through the courtyard, circling columns and doubling back around fountains, until it led them into the castle itself and up to a long flight of stairs.

"Please pick up the pace!" the dodo squawked. "The revisers are nipping at our heels."

Sabrina glanced back and found that the dodo was correct. Her party had gained at least thirty knights, courtiers, and princesses, all of whom were chased by the ravenous monsters. Sabrina watched them—they bounced around like jackals, chomping on everything in their way. What they consumed vanished, only to be replaced with a white nothingness. To call it a hole wouldn't be accurate—what the monsters were doing was eliminating reality, in essence rubbing it out of existence like an eraser. Watching it was the scariest thing Sabrina had ever seen. No wonder the dodo was panicked.

They soon reached the top of the stairs and raced down a long passageway. At the end they found the ball sputtering and rolling against a huge wooden door. Daphne tried the knob, but it was locked.

"Hey, Arthur, you have a key to this door?" she shouted back to the king.

"I'm afraid not," the king said. "These are Sir Gawain's quarters. He has decided to stay in the story."

"I can get us through the door, but you must take me with you," a voice said from the back of the crowd. A small figure pushed its way to the front. It was Pinocchio.

"You!" Sabrina cried.

"I really can get that door open. Do we have a deal?"

Daphne nodded. "Do it."

Pinocchio reached into his pocket and took out a pin. He slid it into the lock and twisted and turned until it clicked. "A little trick I learned while living on the streets of Italy," he said.

He pushed the door open. In the room beyond was a second door, this one standing upright in the middle of the room. Unfortunately, Mirror was standing in front of it.

"I knew we couldn't trust you," Sabrina said to the boy.

"I swear I had no clue he was here," Pinocchio said.

"Just wait. His nose will grow," Daphne said. "It happens when he tells a lie."

"Give me the boy, Sabrina," Mirror demanded, cutting off the bickering.

Sabrina shook her head and struggled with her squirming brother. "He's not yours. He belongs with us."

Mirror's face turned purple with anger. The veins in his neck popped out and his eyes grew dark. "Those creatures will be here at any moment. Once they arrive, they will devour this room and everyone in it, including the boy."

"Then get out of the way and we'll leave."

"They're coming!" the dodo shouted. "You can stand and argue all you want. Just open the door and let us through."

"I agree," Sir Lancelot shouted. "Your dispute does not involve us. Step aside and let us pass."

"Then we have a dilemma," Mirror said. "I want the child. You want to pass. I'll let everyone through this door if one of you brings me my boy."

"Hand him over," the Cheshire Cat cried. "He will still be alive, as will we. What good is there in letting us all die?"

Puck drew his sword, but his arm shook from the earlier blasts. "I will run through the first person who even thinks of trying." His weakened state sapped the necessary intimidation from the threat.

The first reviser scurried into the room. Its sharp little teeth chomped and gnashed. Then it sprang at Sir Lancelot. The knight fought fiercely, swinging his sword at the monster, but the reviser was fast and agile. It leaped out of the way of Lancelot's attacks until it sank its teeth into the man's sword. A second later, the sword was gone. Three more revisers sprang into the room and jumped on Lancelot, the dodo, and King Arthur.

"It's the only way to save his life, Starfish," Mirror said with open arms.

"Daddy!" the boy cried.

Sabrina felt faint and flushed. Her head was turning like a top. What should she do? What was the right choice?

"Give him to Mirror," a voice said. Sabrina turned, ready to throttle whoever had spoken. She was surprised to find it was Daphne.

Reluctantly, Sabrina held out her brother to Mirror. She had no choice.

"We will stop him. We'll have another chance," Daphne said.

"I have no doubt you will try," Mirror said as the toddler hugged him. Mirror paid little mind to his affection. He held him the way one might a sack of groceries. He opened the door and stepped into the angry wind, and then he was gone.

"Clearly that was the responsible choice," the White Rabbit said.

If Sabrina could kill someone with a look, the rabbit would have died on the spot. "Get through the door," she shouted. "Every last cowardly one of you!"

The crowd rushed past her and fled into the empty void of the door. Puck snatched Pinocchio by his collar.

"You're sticking with me, toothpick," he said as the little boy fought to escape his grip. Pinocchio's hand shot into his pocket and the fairy godmother wand came out. He flicked it and it lit up like a firecracker. A blast came out that narrowly missed Puck's foot. Unfortunately, it hit the ball of magic yarn instead. The ball let out a little yelp and smoke came out of it.

Daphne reached down and snatched the ball. "If you busted this, you're in deep trouble." She tried to take the magic wand from Pinocchio but he squirmed free and jumped through the portal before anyone could stop him.

At that moment, Sabrina couldn't have cared less about him.

"Just go!" she said as a tear dropped from her cheek. She followed the others through the door. The last thing Sabrina saw was the gnashing teeth of the revisers.

• • •

Sabrina found herself inside a tiny horse-drawn coach packed to its roof with children. Her group's sudden appearance triggered a massive groan from the already crowded kids as they were shoved violently into smaller and tighter corners of the coach. Sabrina had never had claustrophobia before, but at that moment she felt trapped and unable to breathe.

"Sabrina!" Daphne's voice cried out from somewhere in the mob.

"I'm here," Sabrina said, choking. She tried to turn, but dozens of bodies were pressing against her. It felt like being locked inside a coffin or buried alive. She could feel panic coming on like a typhoon and her stomach was swirling uncomfortably. "Stay calm," she told herself.

"Where are we?" the Cheshire Cat said, shoving the crowd for a little space. His efforts tumbled the children back and forth.

"And where's Pinocchio?" Daphne asked.

"I see him," Puck said from somewhere behind Sabrina. "He's outside the coach, near the driver."

Sabrina pushed against the mob of children and peered

between the bars separating the coach from the front of the vehicle. She spotted a short, fat tub of a man who was wider than he was tall sitting with his back to her. His appearance was almost inhuman—more like a drawing of how a person might look than an actual person. The strange driver rode atop a buckboard and steered a team of skinny donkeys. Sitting next to him was Pinocchio.

"What story are we in?" Sabrina called out to him.

"Mine," Pinocchio said. The smile on his face was not reassuring.

"Uh-oh," Daphne said.

"I have to get out of here," Sabrina said as she pulled on the bars that lined the coach. She fought desperately, letting out a terrified scream, and then everything turned a milky gray and flashed black . . .

When she woke, she saw her sister above her and a crowd of concerned faces gathered around. She was no longer in the coach. She was lying on a cold, cobblestone street.

"What happened?" she said, trying to sit up. Her eyes felt like they were rolling in their sockets, so she lay back down for a moment.

"You fainted," Daphne said.

"Where's Pinocchio?" she asked.

Daphne pointed down the street toward a little town. She saw a banner that read WELCOME TO TOYLAND.

Sabrina craned her neck for a better view and saw a bizarre little town lined with multicolored houses and streets littered with discarded toys. Everywhere she looked there were children running and playing without a care in the world. The biggest house on the street was under attack by an army of children dressed in tinfoil armor. A boy dressed in a king's robes and a cardboard crown stood on the roof waving a paper sword and laughing at the approaching army. His soldiers below him were pelting them with water balloons and eggs.

"Just rest," Daphne said.

Sabrina forced herself to her feet. "We can't. We have to turn him over to the Editor."

Daphne looked concerned as she took out the ball of yarn. She said Pinocchio's name into it and set it on the ground. It popped and fizzled, but would not roll forward.

"That magic-wand blast must have fried it," Daphne said. "I think we should leave it alone for a while—give it time to cool off."

Sabrina frowned and took a few deep breaths. "Then we'll do this the old-fashioned way. We should split up. Arthur, Lancelot, Guinevere—take a few of the other knights. You're in one group. Puppy, rabbit, cat, dodo—take some knights with you, too. My sister and Puck and I will stick together." She didn't want anyone slowing them down.

"I must protest your plan," the White Rabbit said. "What if we do not find one another again? Any number of things could happen while we are here. One of us could become injured—or we could get lost. We would be trapped here."

"I couldn't care less," Sabrina said. "We're not babysitting you."

Daphne raised her hands to calm the group. "Rabbit, you're the one with the pocket watch. Meet us back here in an hour. And everyone else, do yourself a favor and don't play with any of the kids in the town. Playing is a bad thing."

"The words you say are insane," Puck said. "They come out of your mouth like regular words but make no sense."

"Every kid on this island is going to turn into a donkey," Daphne explained, pointing to the beasts that had pulled them in the coach. "The driver will sell them all to farms, where they will be worked to death."

"She's right," said a boy who, unlike the others from the wagon, had stayed behind when the rest rushed into the town. "Pinocchio gets sent to a circus to be trained as a dancing donkey. I end up on a farm where I die."

"How do you know?" the Cheshire Cat purred.

"I'm Lampwick, his best friend." The boy started to run off to join the other children.

"Wait! Where are you going?" Sabrina said. "If you know you're going to die, why not turn around and go home?"

The boy shook his head. "The Editor would not approve."

"Then join our army," Arthur said. "We're traveling through the stories. Soon we'll find a door to the real world and we'll escape for good. You could be free."

Lampwick smiled and shook his head. "And then what? I have a role here. I'm important to Pinocchio's development. When he witnesses my death as a broken-down farm animal, it has a profound effect on him. Without me, his efforts to become a good boy might never occur. Even though I have a small part in his life, I'm essential to its direction."

"You're a fool!" the dodo said.

"I'm part of his growth as a character," the boy said. "It is my tragic end that makes him a better person. In any good story the hero must experience tragedy to grow and ultimately defeat what is destroying him. I know the story isn't called 'Lampwick,' but I'm arguably the most important character in it."

And with that, the boy disappeared into the throng of kids.

"I've heard enough of his nonsense," the White Rabbit said.

"Come on, now. Let's find your Pinocchio and get out of here."

The three groups walked in different directions, and with each step Sabrina felt more and more overcome with grief and panic. The claustrophobia came back to her tenfold and she fell to her knees, sobbing.

"Sabrina!" Daphne said, trying to help her up.

"What did I do, Daphne? I gave him back to Mirror!"

"I told you to! We had no choice," Daphne said.

Sabrina ignored her. "How could I do that?"

"He was going to let people die," Daphne said.

"What if we don't get him back?"

There was silence for a long time.

"We will get him back," Puck said. "I will make sure of it."

Sabrina looked up into his face, fully prepared to insult the boy, but instead she saw a determination in Puck that seemed genuine. Every hint of sarcasm was gone. Even the playful gleam in his eyes had been snuffed out. "You sacrificed him for us all, including me. I will repay that debt. No harm will come to your brother. The Trickster King makes this vow."

"You're not alone here, Sabrina," Daphne added. "We're here. We're a team. And we all would have done the same thing. You heard the Editor. Mirror's story is off-limits. He can't get into it, so whatever he has planned for Carmine can't be done anyway."

"Carmine?" Puck said.

Daphne rolled her eyes. "Fine, Baby X is his name! Are you two happy?"

Sabrina couldn't help but laugh. "Baby X is worse than Carmine."

Daphne laughed, as did Puck. It was nice to see smiles again, and Sabrina started to think things might be all right.

"All right, enough of the boo-boo faces," Puck said. "Let's get back to work. There will be plenty of time for personal disappointments when we get married."

"It sounds charming," Sabrina said. "But that's also why I would never marry you no matter what!"

"Sorry," Puck chuckled. "Fate has us forever intertwined."

Sabrina rolled her eyes. "Daphne, you said you've read this story. Fill us in on what we're missing."

"I know that eventually Pinocchio turns into a donkey. Then he gets sold to the circus. Then his owner tries to drown him in the ocean—"

"That's nice!" Sabrina interjected. "What kind of children's story is this?"

"Then a fisherman catches him, I think. He might live with the Blue Fairy for a while, then he gets eaten by a shark. There are lots of twists and turns."

Daphne was still trying to figure out the order of the events when the puppy dog leaped out in front of them. "We found him! C'mon!"

The children chased after the giant dog as he weaved through the senseless maze of Toyland's streets. They faced one obstacle after another. On one street they had to duck back and find another path as they almost ran into a group of children playing a game to see who could shatter the biggest window in a large church. The stained-glass shards came down like razor-sharp rainbows and there was no way to pass safely.

Another street had a group of children in the midst of a makeshift jousting tournament. Two children rode donkeys at each other and took turns trying to knock their opponent off with pillows. They also saw a little boy who had uncovered a can of green paint and was stalking around like a giggling idiot drenching anyone who came within five feet of him.

After many failed efforts, Sabrina and her family managed to find a clear path to a filthy tent. Once inside, Sabrina spotted the driver of the coach standing next to a trembling donkey.

"He's selling the animals," the Cheshire Cat said when they joined him and the others in the tent.

"Disgusting practice," the White Rabbit complained.

"Pinocchio has already turned into a donkey?" Sabrina asked.

"He couldn't have. I remember the story said he was here for weeks before the change started," Daphne said.

The Cheshire Cat motioned to a dark section of the tent. "He's over there. I can see well in the dark. He's hiding in the shadows."

"Why?" Lancelot asked.

"Pinocchio winds up in a circus, so he has to be sold. Maybe he's trying to hurry everything along," Daphne said. "He's watching for the Ringmaster and he'll stow himself away when he leaves."

"How much will you give me for this fine, strong donkey?" the fat man said. His voice was high and piercing.

"I'll take him for twenty-five nickels," a man said. "I can use his skin for a drum I have at home."

The donkey brayed and whimpered until the fat man snapped his whip at him.

"Do I hear more than twenty-five nickels?"

"Does he dance?" another man shouted from the crowd.

"Pardon?"

A man dressed in a long black coat, white pants, and black boots stood up. "Does he dance? I have a circus in need of an act," the man replied. "If he can dance, I'll pay fifty nickels."

"You're a ringmaster, I see. You could teach him to dance in your circus," the fat man said.

"NO! He must dance. I won't pay for a donkey that doesn't dance."

Suddenly Pinocchio stepped into the light. "He dances," he said. "Like a prima ballerina. I've seen him myself."

The fat man and the Ringmaster were confused. "You must follow the actual events."

"This is my story," Pinocchio said. "Take the donkey to your circus. I will accompany you."

"Does the Editor know about this?" another man in the crowd asked.

Pinocchio removed the magic wand from his pants pocket. He flicked it with his wrist and a blue flame ignited the air. "The Editor knows what I've told him," he said. The men were taken aback by the magic. "Now, if you have sufficiently eaten up the oxygen in this tent with your stupid questions, can we get on with it?"

The fat man nodded. "Take him with you, Ringmaster."

The crowd stood all at once and in the excitement Sabrina lost sight of the little troublemaker. One moment he was standing in the center of everything and the next he was gone.

"Find him!" Sabrina shouted to the characters, and they all raced out of the tent. Without the magic yarn ball they had to ask everyone they came across for help. They went from building to building asking children if they had seen Pinocchio, but all the children were caught up in their games or were intentionally rude. Most of them stuck their tongues out at Sabrina or tried to pelt her with crab apples.

"Little kids are jerks," Sabrina said.

"Um, hello?" Daphne said with mock offense.

"Except you," Sabrina said. "He's gone. What do we do?"

"In the story, he is sold to the circus. The Blue Fairy shows up at one of the shows," Daphne said. "It's his chance to get her to fix the spell that turned him into a real boy."

"How are we going to find a traveling circus?" Guinevere complained.

"I don't know exactly, but the first step is getting out of this town," Daphne said. "If we stick around, we're all going to be eating hay and swatting at flies with our tails."

"She's right," Sabrina said. "He's not here anymore anyway. It's better to leave while we can."

The group walked through the town gate and spotted a crude sign outside that read TOYS ARE GRATE! NO MORE SKOOLS! DOWN WITH RITT MATTICK!

"Hey, where you going?" a girl missing a front tooth said as the group departed the town. "It's dangerous to go into the parts of the story that aren't written. The margins are full of ghosties."

"We're running away to join the circus," Sabrina said. She walked on, leaving behind the troubling little town and its doomed population. Soon it was just a speck of dust on the horizon.

• • •

They walked along the road for what seemed the better part of a day. By the time they decided to make a camp for the night, Sabrina was sure she would collapse from exhaustion, pain, and hunger. She realized she hadn't eaten all day.

King Arthur took his men into the woods, promising to find some game for dinner. The White Rabbit insisted they not hunt any of his brothers or sisters, and the dodo demanded that whatever they brought back not be an endangered species. Meanwhile, the rest of the Wonderland refugees trotted off in search of water and fruit. Daphne and Puck collected some firewood and stones to build a campfire.

Sabrina wanted to help, but she felt beaten and ill. Her hip was throbbing and her head felt like a demolition site. She closed her eyes, trying to block out the pain, and she must have fallen asleep, because when she opened them again she found a wild boar roasting above a crackling fire. The sun had vanished and the stars were like little pinpricks on a black canvas. Plus her hunger had turned ravenous. When the boar was ready, she ate like a starving coyote and drank more than her share of the sweet water the Cheshire Cat had brought back to the camp via the knights' helmets. With her belly full and her thirst quenched, she was surprised to find that she didn't feel that much better. In fact, she was still terribly exhausted. She hobbled over to a patch of softer ground and called her sister to her side.

"I need to rest," she said apologetically. "You're in charge. Don't let them talk you into moving on. Don't let them bully you either. If you have to get Puck to turn into a dragon or something to threaten them—do it."

Sabrina wouldn't remember if Daphne agreed or not. A moment later, she fell into a sleep that was deep, dark, and dreamless.

Sometime in the night she awoke with a pain in her side; a terrible blow rocked her body. She scampered backward, only to find that she was the only one in her group who was awake. The others had settled in for the night and the campfire was now a fading orange glow of embers. She would have thought the blow had been a dream except for the sharp pain in her ribs. She pulled up her shirt and found a growing purple bruise. Something had struck her. She was not imagining it.

She wondered if something had fallen from the tree above and hit her, but there was nothing. Perhaps some wild animal had come along and tried to take a bite, then darted off when she woke. Whatever the case, she knew that sleeping was now out of the question.

She saw something move in the woods to her left, and then it appeared on the right. It was just a flash and could have easily been a trick of the light, but then there was something standing over her. It wasn't so much a person as it was the faint notion of the form of a person—mostly invisible but swirling with dust and dirt like a tiny hurricane trapped in a human-shaped shell.

"What are you?" Sabrina asked.

"Free me," it croaked. Then whatever it was vanished.

• • •

The morning came and the ragtag group filled their bellies with some wild grapes and a few unidentifiable fish the cat caught in the stream. They cooked them over a fresh fire, and then they picked up their search for Pinocchio.

"You've been quiet all morning," Daphne told Sabrina.

Sabrina didn't want to frighten her sister with thoughts of ghosts. They had plenty of things to worry about as it was. "I just want to find Pinocchio as soon as we can."

After nearly another whole day of walking, they came across a little town. It would have been nothing more than a place to pass through if not for the huge sign tacked to a tree.

GRAND GALA SHOW
This evening
WITNESS THE TROUPE'S USUAL
AMAZING LEAPS & FEATS
PERFORMED BY ALL ITS ARTISTS
& all its horses, mares, and stallions alike,
plus
appearing for the first time
the famous
DONKEY PINOCCHIO
also known as
THE STAR OF THE DANCE
The theater will be as bright as day

Puck stopped an old man who was hobbling down the road, powered only by his cane and stubbornness. The old man told him the theater was at the other end of the town but not before he gave him a good swat with his cane. He apparently objected to Puck calling him "gramps."

They dashed to the theater box office, but with no money they were forced to barter. Eventually, after much begging, Sabrina convinced King Arthur to part with his crown, insisting that when they got to the real world he would no longer be royalty anyway. The crown got them all front-row seats as well as a few nickels to spend at the local grocer. Unfortunately, there wasn't enough money in the world to shut the king up about the indignity suffered. He claimed he felt naked without it and kept worrying about having "crown head."

Eventually the doors to the theater opened and the crowd entered the venue. Everyone found their seats and waited for the show to begin. Meanwhile, Sabrina, Puck, and Daphne searched the crowd for signs of Pinocchio or the Blue Fairy.

"You're sure the Blue Fairy shows up in this part of the story?" Sabrina asked her sister.

Daphne nodded. "If he's going to make his move, it will be tonight."

"I have a few ideas I'd like to run past you about how we plan to stop him," Puck said. "First, I was thinking I could clobber him with a chair. It happens all the time on television and seems fairly effective."

"Let's just try to grab him without smashing furniture over his head," Sabrina said.

Several horns played a happy tune and the audience applauded. The Ringmaster came out dressed in a long black jacket, white pants, and knee-high black boots. He bowed deeply. In the blazing theater lights he looked bewildered, almost frightened. He reminded Sabrina of Mikey Beiterman, a budding actor in her second-grade class. During her school's production of *Little Shop of Horrors*, he had forgotten what he was supposed to say. A teacher had attempted to whisper the line to him, but he was so embarrassed he burst into tears and ran backstage, refusing to return for the rest of the play. Unfortunately, Mikey was playing the part of the man-eating plant and was crucial to the next two acts. The Ringmaster had the same lost expression on his face. "Ladies and gentlemen, I'm afraid the act advertised tonight featuring Pinocchio the dancing donkey has been canceled. Instead, I offer you the amazing Russian Stallion Brigade."

Several white stallions trotted onstage led by two beautiful identical twins. They marched the stallions to one end of the stage, then the other.

The audience murmured until a little boy stood up and cried, "That's not how the story goes. Bring out Pinocchio!"

The audience cheered their approval.

"I can't," the Ringmaster said. "Pinocchio is changing the story. He has not become a donkey. He threatened me."

"Where is he?" Sabrina said, jumping to her feet.

"There!" the man said, pointing at a seat in the upper deck. Sabrina craned her neck to see a woman with bright blue hair being led out of her seat by a young boy. The boy had a magic wand in his hand that glowed like fire.

The crowd cried out in surprise.

"He's got the Blue Fairy!" Sabrina shouted to her friends and they all rushed out of the tent and into the street. There they found Pinocchio glowering at the Blue Fairy.

"Stay out of this," Pinocchio said as the group approached.

"We're not going to let you do this, puppet boy," Daphne said.

"I wasn't a puppet! I was a marionette!"

"Pinocchio! What on earth has gotten into you? I'm like your mother in this story," the Blue Fairy said.

"My mother? I suffered greatly and you didn't lift a finger to help. I was turned into a donkey. I spent a week in the belly of a shark! Two murderers tried to hang me from a tree outside your house. A man tried to drown me. What did you do, O mother dear? Nothing. You're the most powerful Everafter of them all and you did nothing!"

"I understand your anger," the fairy said, "but it is misdirected. I am a storybook portrait of the Blue Fairy. The real Blue Fairy is somewhere in the real world. Whatever your intentions are with me they will not satisfy your need for revenge. I have no idea why my real-life counterpart chose to behave the way she did. But there must be a reason. Perhaps you should go to her for answers."

"No! She will feed me the same mumbo jumbo she always has and will continue to deny me. The Book of Everafter is my only hope. Its power is at my disposal, as are you!" Pinocchio said. "I want to be a man."

Puck stepped forward and Pinocchio turned his wand on him. "You stay back, you filthy street urchin. I have suffered long enough. I will have my wish."

Puck looked back at the group of people with him. "There's a lot of us and only one of you."

"I'll shoot you with this. I swear," he said, his hand trembling with nerves. "I went easy on you before, fairy."

Sabrina and Daphne joined Puck. "He's right. You could manage to get off one shot, maybe two, but you can't hit us all."

"You don't know the fairy godmother wand that well. You've gotten lucky," Daphne added.

Soon Arthur, the knights, and the Wonderland group were standing right behind the children.

"I warned you!" Pinocchio said, flicking the wand. A bolt of energy burst from it and hit Sir Galahad in the chest. There was a pop, a puff of smoke, and then Galahad turned into a turtle.

"I think I know this wand well enough." Pinocchio looked smug.

"Get him!" Puck shouted, and the crowd rushed at Pinocchio. There were more explosions from the wand but soon someone snatched it out of the little boy's hands and he was defenseless. He screamed, cursed, and threatened, but when the dust settled he was on the ground with his hands behind his back. Sabrina had never seen anyone so angry in her life.

"How dare you!" he shouted. "I have a right to live like a normal person. I have a right to grow up!"

Sabrina stood over him as Daphne sat on his back. "I might have thought the same thing, once. But you betrayed us. You were our friend and you sold us out to Mirror. Don't tell me what you are owed. Whatever the Editor chooses to do with you is exactly what you deserve. Hey, Editor! We've got him!"

Just then, a door materialized from thin air and it swung open. Standing in a brilliant light was the Editor.

"Good news, boss. We stopped the puppet," Daphne said.

"These characters do not belong in this story!" the Editor said coolly.

"They followed us," Sabrina said. "We've been—"

"They will have to go back!"

Suddenly Arthur drew his sword and charged at the Editor. The skinny old man fell backward, and the king raced through the doorway after him. The rest of his ragtag army followed. Puck pulled Pinocchio to his feet and they chased the group through the door to the library, trying to convince everyone to stay calm.

"So, you are the vile monster who torments us!" Arthur shouted at the Editor. Murder was in his eyes.

"Stay away from me!" the Editor demanded.

"Women and children, shield your eyes," Arthur commanded. "Blood will soon spill from this man's veins."

7

he group's sudden arrival in the library seemed to make the revisers skittish. They scurried up onto the walls and climbed higher and higher. In his efforts to stay away from King Arthur, the Editor knocked his leather chair over. With the help of Puck, who still held Pinocchio with his other hand, Sabrina pulled the king off of the Editor and positioned herself between them.

"Step aside!" Arthur demanded.

"Put your sword away!" Sabrina shouted twice as loud. Arthur studied her closely and after a very tense moment did as she asked.

"What is this place?" the White Rabbit said, hopping around in an agitated manner.

"This is his library. It's where he devises his plots against us!" Lancelot said.

The Editor scowled. "I do no such thing. My job is to maintain order in this book. I have no interest in plotting against you."

"Arthur, unloose that sword and run him through," Sir Port said.

"I said, leave him alone!" Sabrina demanded.

"Don't pretend to be concerned for me, traitors," the Editor snapped. "You brought your revolution to my doorstep."

"What? We are not part of any revolution," Sabrina said.

The Editor turned his attention to the king. "So, Arthur, not content to be a character in a book anymore?"

"Not content in the least," Arthur said.

"And the rest of you feel the same way?"

The crowd shouted in agreement.

"I suppose all of you think that you deserve freedom? You probably see yourselves as real people with lives to pursue?"

"Indeed," the dodo said. "We no longer can live in this book, doing the same things over and over again. We want out into the real world."

The Editor laughed. What started out as a chuckle turned into an out-of-control guffaw and a stream of tears running down his face.

"What's so funny?" Sir Lancelot barked.

"You! All of you! You think you're real. You aren't any

more real than I am—you're fuzzy memories of events that happened hundreds of years ago. You are not the real King Arthur and you are not the real White Rabbit—you're nothing more than storybook characters walking around pretending to have feelings. You are recollections and notions put down in words and sentences powered by a little bit of magic. You are a portrait, and often times, a failed portrait, of an actual someone. You're not even a shadow lying at the foot of the person you represent."

The crowd booed him.

Pinocchio struggled forward. "I am not with these fools. I am from the real world, and I wish to alter my story. I am shocked and dismayed that you sent the Grimms to prevent it. I must protest and demand you give me my due."

"Your due? You don't have any right to change your story. This book was intended to give your kind a stroll through the good old days and nothing more. It's not for you to meddle with willy-nilly. Do you know what has to be done when you change something? The entire event has to be rewritten, like a story, with a new plot, new themes, new villains! To keep the history running smoothly, every tiny detail must be altered so it fits with the change. If it doesn't make sense, the consequences could be disastrous. You could unravel time itself."

The Editor straightened his tweed suit jacket. "There will be no more changes. These memories, stories, whatever you want to call them, just can't take it. They're not built for re-imagining. You will have to stay the way you are or find another solution. The Book of Everafter is closed for business."

"Enough!" Guinevere shouted. "We have no interest in changing who we are. All we want is out! We know you can open a door to the real world."

"It's a simple request. Just do it and we will let you live," her husband added.

"Do you think that I respond to your demands? I am the Editor. I control this book."

"You are mistaken, sir," Lancelot said. "We have minds and desires, and we will not take part in your game any longer."

"Sadly, there is only one thing I can do, then," the Editor said.

"You will free us?" Arthur said.

"No, Your Majesty. I believe it's time you were edited," he said, raising his hands above his head.

Just then, there was a loud scurrying sound as if all the world's cockroaches were marching toward them. Sabrina looked to the ceiling and saw hundreds of revisers crawling down the bookshelves. Some of them jumped down and landed on the characters, digging their angry teeth into arms and legs. The knights were more prepared to fight than the maidens and talking animals, but most of the members of the so-called Character Liberation Army were unarmed and had no experience in battle. It wasn't long before they were erased from existence by the pink creatures.

Pinocchio turned to Sabrina. "Get me out of here!" he demanded.

Sabrina scanned the room and saw a door materializing. She threw it open and felt a damp, chilly breeze brush against her face.

"Where does it go?" the boy asked.

"Does it matter?" Puck said as he raised his foot and kicked the little boy in the behind. Pinocchio flew face-first through the void and vanished.

Sabrina pulled Daphne toward the door and ushered her through.

"Take me!" the White Rabbit shouted. He hopped through, leaving his companions behind. The Cheshire Cat attempted the same move, but the revisers leaped onto him. He cried out for help, but soon he was gone—and nothing more than a memory. The puppy was next, though he did manage to bite a reviser in half in his desperate struggle. Its insides were spongy and solid, just like its body, with no blood or bones, nothing to show that it was alive. But there were too many others and the puppy was outnumbered. Guinevere followed, falling under a mass of monsters. Lancelot rushed over; his love for her clearly transcended what was written about him. He tried to fight them back but soon he was overwhelmed too.

"We have to go!" Puck shouted. "But I have to tell you, Grimm. We have to start carrying a camera with us. This would be an awesome addition to my scrapbooking project."

"Scrapbooking?" Sabrina said.

Puck blushed. "Evil scrapbooking."

He stepped though the doorway and vanished.

Sabrina lingered until she caught the Editor's eye. "This was not our fault." She hoped he might believe her. She needed his help to stop Mirror. But his face was as cold as stone. The nightmare of the revisers chomping all around him looked as if it were a tedious chore—like washing dishes or vacuuming a rug. His was not the face of a man in the midst of a massacre.

The Editor shook his head. "You're on your own now."

"But—"

"You marched an army into my sanctuary. They planned to kill me if I didn't give them what they wanted, and you expect me to help you now?"

Defeated, she backed into the doorway. The last thing she saw were the Editor's bored eyes watching his creatures clean up her mess.

• • •

Sabrina found herself atop a horse in the middle of an old country road. Before her was a wooden bridge spanning a small brook. The moon shone down on the water and its reflection danced like a ballerina. Stars looked like faraway flashlights. As she was from New York City, Sabrina hadn't seen many real stars until she moved to Ferryport Landing. But this sky was even more magnificent. It was completely undisturbed by artificial light.

"Where are we?" Pinocchio asked.

"I don't know," Daphne said. She was standing next to the horse along with Pinocchio and the White Rabbit. "But it seems familiar."

Sabrina scanned the woods. Things did look familiar to her. The trees were like those in Ferryport Landing. She spotted several oaks and cedars. Even the air smelled like home. Still, things seemed slightly out of focus. "Could we be back home?"

"Not unless you dress like that all the time," Puck said.

Sabrina looked down at herself. She was wearing short black pants, white leggings, a heavy wool cloak, a shirt with a stiff white collar, and a dusted wig.

"It could be any story. They're almost all set in forests," Daphne said. "But this seems oddly familiar."

Just then, the horse let out a horrible whinny and reared back on its legs. Sabrina, who had never ridden a horse except for on the carousel in Central Park, grabbed its reins and struggled to stay in the saddle. The horse stomped around, snorting and whimpering.

"What's wrong?" Sabrina wondered.

"Maybe he got a whiff of you," Puck teased.

"He sees something," the White Rabbit said. "Something out in the dark has frightened him. Perhaps it's the villain, Mirror."

"There!" Daphne cried as she pointed at a figure across the bridge. Sabrina strained her eyes and saw a black figure sitting atop a black horse. She couldn't make out his features, but there was something wrong about him. His body was misshapen.

"Who are you?" Sabrina cried out, but the figure did not reply. What if it was the phantom living in the margins of the stories?

"That's kind of rude of him," Daphne said.

Suddenly the figure and its horse charged the bridge, coming to a halt midway across. The sudden movement startled Sabrina's mount and it took all her strength and balance to get it back under control. It also made her mad.

"Listen, man. You are freaking out my horse, so cut it out with all the creepy spastic stuff," Sabrina said.

The figure did not respond.

"I'm warning you, pal. You do it again and I'm going to knock your block off!"

The figure edged his horse closer and stopped in a beam of moonlight. There its horrible shape revealed itself. The horse had eyes filled with flickering flames and a sulfuric smoke blasted out of its nostrils. Its rider wore what appeared to be an ancient military uniform, but whether it was a man or a woman was impossible to tell, as the figure did not have a head. A chill ran through Sabrina. She had been face-to-face with lots of creatures one might call monsters but all of them had heads.

"I know what story we're in," Daphne said as the figure drew a long, silver sword from his sheath. "This is 'The Legend of Sleepy Hollow.' That's why the trees look familiar. This is set in upstate New York—less than fifty miles from Ferryport Landing. That dude is the Headless Horseman."

"Get on the horse," Sabrina demanded.

"Did you hear me?" Daphne said. "I know the story."

"I heard you. Get on the horse!"

Puck snatched the little girl from under her arms and hoisted her onto the horse.

"I'm assuming the plan is to run," Puck said.

Sabrina clenched the horse's reins tight in her hands. "Any pointers on riding a horse?"

"It's easy once you get them started," the boy fairy said.

"And how do I do that?"

Puck raised his hand and smacked the horse in the behind so hard it sounded like a thunderclap. The horse squealed and took off like a shot. Sabrina and Daphne were bounced around like Ping-Pong balls but held on to the horse with all their strength. All the while, the black menace followed from behind.

"They should put seat belts on this thing," Daphne cried. "If we don't slow it down, we're going to fall off."

"But if we slow it down, he's going to get us!" Sabrina shouted.

Just then, Puck zipped by with his wings flapping furiously. Pinocchio hung from below, complaining about his "man-handling."

"Where's the White Rabbit?" Daphne asked.

Puck shrugged. "He refused to come, so I left him—something about being afraid to fly. Hey! Did you know that guy chasing us doesn't have a head?"

"Maybe that's why they call him the Headless Horseman!" Sabrina shouted.

"I bet that hurt," Puck said, almost as if he respected the spooky figure. "I wonder what happened to it."

"Uh, it's right there!" Daphne cried as she pointed back to the monster.

Sabrina craned her neck and saw the Headless Horseman removing a ghostly, freaky head from its saddlebag. It was wrapped in filthy rags.

"Sabrina, stop!" Daphne said, pulling hard on the reins. Their horse skidded to a stop on the pebbled path. A second later, the Headless Horseman's head flew past them, sailing into the woods and rolling down an embankment. If the girls hadn't stopped their horse, it would have hit them for sure.

"Did he just throw his head at you?" Puck cried. "'Cause that is totally awesome. Wait a minute. I just got a great idea for centerpieces at our reception . . ."

The Headless Horseman stopped for a moment as if confused, and then he steered his horse off the road and down the embankment.

"That was the most deplorable experience of my life," Pinocchio complained. "I have never been so poorly treated."

"Never, really?" Puck said. "I'm so proud of myself."

"Uh-oh," Daphne said.

"What's uh-oh," Sabrina asked.

"The ball of yarn is missing," Daphne said, searching through her pockets.

"Maybe it fell on the road during the chase," Sabrina said, scanning the ground beneath her. There was nothing but fallen leaves and the occasional mouse.

"I need a closer look." Daphne climbed off the horse, as did Sabrina. They slowly walked back the way they came.

"Aren't you three concerned about the fellow with the missing head?" Pinocchio said. "What if he comes back?"

"I've read the story," Daphne said. "We're at the end. He's probably waiting there until it starts over. Sabrina, I'm not seeing it."

"This is all very tedious," Pinocchio complained. "I don't see why I should have to assist you in your search. Set me down by a tree and come back for me when you have found your trinket."

Sabrina ignored the boy. She was too busy fighting off a panic attack. Without that ball of yarn they might never find their way out of the Book. They would never find Mirror and the baby, either. If the revisers appeared, as they should at any moment, they would be in even more trouble.

"I've got an idea," Puck said. He spun around on his heels and in a very troubling metamorphosis his head transformed into a bloodhound's. He got down on his hands and knees and snorted at the ground. Then he hopped back up and ran down the path. Sabrina spotted a bushy tail poking out of the back of his pants. It wagged back and forth like an excited windshield wiper.

"I think he has picked up a scent," Daphne said, running after him. Sabrina abandoned the horse and shoved Pinocchio along ahead of her. Puck darted off into the woods, racing along the bubbling creek, under the bridge where the ground was thick with mud, and then up an embankment littered with slippery leaves. They spotted a door not far ahead, but they also saw something that made her equally nervous. The White Rabbit was chasing after the ball of yarn as it rolled toward the magical door.

"I thought it was broken," Sabrina said.

"I did too!" Daphne exclaimed.

The rabbit glanced back at them and doubled his speed, and soon he had scooped up the yarn and was opening the door. The wind blasted leaves back into his little face.

"I'm sorry!" he called when the children approached. "I have to take this chance while it's in front of me. You are slowing me down and I won't end up like the others."

"We need that ball of yarn," Sabrina said. "It's the only way we'll find our baby brother. And maybe the only way we'll find our way out of this book."

The White Rabbit shook his head. "I wish you luck." And then he darted through the open doorway. It slammed shut and vanished into thin air, taking him and the magic ball of yarn with it.

• • •

They sat still, trying to be patient.

"I've got to find somewhere to go to the bathroom," Daphne said. She was prancing around and looked distressed.

"Daphne, it's too dangerous."

"But I have to!" Daphne cried. "It's an emergency."

She looked to Puck. The fairy laughed. "Don't look to me for help. I'm having a great time watching your silly dance."

"Please! If you don't let me go, something bad is going to happen," the little girl begged.

Sabrina sighed. "Don't go far and come—"

Before Sabrina could finish the little girl darted off like a roadrunner.

"—right back!" Sabrina called after her.

"She can go and I can't!" Pinocchio fumed. Puck had taken the liberty of tying him up using a tree and a roll of duct tape he carried in his pocket. Sabrina couldn't get him to explain why he had duct tape, but then realized the boy's pockets were probably full of emergency prank supplies.

Puck laughed at the little traitor. "You can suffer, ugly. Besides, I'm not sure I can even get you out of your bindings.

The marshmallow told me I was using too much tape, but it was so funny I couldn't stop. We're probably going to have to leave you here."

"You wouldn't dare!" the boy seethed.

"You don't know him at all," Sabrina said to Pinocchio.

"So," Puck said, turning to Sabrina. "You dropped like a rock back in Pinocchio's story. I thought you had died."

"You wish."

Puck shook his head. "No way! You can't die. I've already sent out 'save the date' cards for the wedding, and I've registered for gifts. If you croak, I'll never get that mayonnaise cannon."

"What store sells a mayonnaise cannon?" Sabrina said, and then shook her head. She didn't really want to know.

"You're not lost," he said suddenly.

"Huh?"

"I know you feel like you don't know what you're doing. All your decisions seem to be wrong. You feel like you're lost, but you're not."

"My decisions seem to be wrong because they *are* wrong," Sabrina said. "I gambled with my baby brother's life. I trusted the White Rabbit and his stupid army. I turned the Editor against us. I lost the magic yarn. I got us hopelessly lost. Worst of all, I wasted all our time and energy on this idiot—"

"You don't have to be rude," Pinocchio said.

"You're right. You make lousy decisions," Puck said. "But you're supposed to. You're the hero."

"Huh?"

"Listen, I've been told tons of stories and there's one thing that they all have in common—the hero has a terrible time. It's what that Lampwick kid said when we were in Pinocchio's story. The hero has to go through all kind of obstacles so that he or she can overcome them. Like me: I have to overcome your smell!"

"My life is not a fairy tale," Sabrina said.

"But you'll have a happy ever after when we get married," Puck said.

"Don't tease me. A person can only take so much bad news."

Puck jumped to his feet. "I'm not happy about a lot of things either, you know. Look at me—I'm one of the good guys now. Worse, I'm thinking about your feelings and not about what kind of gunk I can pour over your head," he complained. "Do you realize how low I've sunk? I'm the Trickster King. I'm the shaman of stupidity, the Dalai Lama of dumb jokes, the holy man of horrible pranks." He sighed forlornly. "Now all of a sudden I'm Mr. Sensitive."

"Sabrina!" Daphne cried as she raced into the clearing.

Sabrina and Puck rushed to her. "What? Were you attacked?"

"What? No, of course not," Daphne said. "I think I know how to get one of those doors to open for us. We have to put together a new ending. The horseman's up on the hill looking for his head. I heard him fumbling around up there."

"You aren't suggesting we confront that devil," Pinocchio said.

"Yes, you have to if we want out of here."

"Me?" Pinocchio looked at the children. "What does this have to do with me?"

 fter unwrapping Pinocchio from his prison of duct tape, the children walked back to the shadow-filled road. The air had turned crisp and chilly and Sabrina could see a puff of water vapor whenever she breathed out.

"What do you want me to do?" Pinocchio said. His tone made it clear that he felt very put out by the request.

"Stand here in the road and taunt the Horseman," Sabrina said.

"And how do I do that?"

"Do what comes naturally," Daphne said. "Be very annoying."

"How dare you!"

"Just stand there and call him names," Sabrina said, ignoring his indignation.

"I hardly think a few insults are going to bother an undead soldier from the depths of the underworld," Pinocchio whined.

"You're right," Puck said. From underneath his hoodie he removed an object wrapped in old rags and handed it to the boy. It was shaped like a small watermelon and smelled foul. "Wave this around."

"What's this?"

"The Horseman's head."

Pinocchio let out a girlish scream and dropped the head.

Puck scooped it off the ground. "Hey! This is valuable."

"You had his head the whole time?" Sabrina asked.

Puck nodded.

"Why?" Daphne said, her eyes as big as saucers.

"It's a souvenir," Puck said. "I was thinking I'd put it on the mantel above the fireplace."

"It's someone's head!" Sabrina cried.

"It's a conversation piece," Puck corrected her, and then shoved it back into Pinocchio's hands. "And I will want it back!"

Pinocchio held the object as far from his body as he could.

"Just shout that you have it," Daphne said to the boy. "According to the story, this guy is obsessed with it. He'll be along pretty fast."

"Great," Pinocchio said through a thick layer of sarcasm.

The children scuttled off to hide in the brush and wait.

Sabrina watched Pinocchio kicking at pebbles and looking around aimlessly. After several moments, she lost her patience with the boy.

"What are you doing?" she whispered.

"My job!" he shouted. "I'm the bait!"

"Make some noise. Be obnoxious. Tease him!"

"At least wave the head around," Puck added.

Pinocchio rolled his eyes and lifted the head over his own. "Hey! Horseman! I got your head. Nah-nah-na-na-nah!" He turned to the children. "Happy?"

"You are worthless," Sabrina said, marching out into the road. She snatched the head from the boy. "Like this! Hey Horseman! You want your head? Too bad! It's mine now. I might use it like a soccer ball or sell it on the Internet. But you can have it back if you want it. All you have to do is take it from me!"

Pinocchio growled. "Sorry if I don't have a lot of experience taunting people with their own body parts."

"You don't have a lot of experience doing anything for anyone else," Sabrina said. "For someone who claims to be an adult trapped in a little boy's body, you act like a baby."

"You insolent brat!" Pinocchio said. "If I was big enough, I'd put you over my knee."

"I'd like to see you try," Sabrina said.

"Hey! Can't you hear that?" Daphne said.

"Hear what?!" Pinocchio and Sabrina shouted.

"The horse hooves! He's coming."

Sabrina stood for a moment. She could hear the beating of a horse on the road.

"You're supposed to hold this!" she cried, forcing the head back into his hands.

"It's too great an honor," Pinocchio said, slamming it back into her hands. "I insist."

Just then, the dark, terrifying figure appeared on the road. His silver sword flashed in the moonlight and fire flickered in his horse's eyes.

"Where's the door?"

"It should appear any second," Daphne replied.

"You better be right," Sabrina said.

Sabrina watched as Pinocchio sprinted away. She tucked the head under her arm and started to chase after him, but only after a few steps she heard Puck's voice shout "No!"

Sabrina turned to find the boy fairy had leaped onto the road with his sword in hand. His sudden appearance caused the horse to reel back. The Headless Horseman lost his balance and flew off, slamming to the ground with a thud.

"Should I give him the head?" Sabrina asked.

"Yes!"

Sabrina tossed the head to the demon, then watched as a door in the road materialized next to her. When Daphne opened it, a fierce gale exploded from the doorway—but a tornado couldn't have held them back. Sabrina, Daphne, Puck, and Pinocchio darted through, the smell of jasmine tea and spices enveloping their senses.

• • •

When Sabrina's vision cleared, she stood in an arid desert and blinked into the brutal sun. Even taking a breath seemed to burn her throat.

"At least it's not a forest," Pinocchio said. "All these woodland stories are doing a number on my allergies."

"Where do you think we are?" Daphne asked.

"Not a clue," Sabrina said as she rolled up her sleeves.

"I think we'll find out in there," Puck said, pointing behind the group. Sabrina turned and saw a slab of marble rising up from the sand. The slab had a golden ring on it and was leaning open, revealing a flight of stairs descending underground. She sighed.

"All right, then," Sabrina said. "Let's get this over with."

The children climbed down the stairs and found themselves

inside a huge subterranean garden. Sabrina had never seen anything like it. Despite the lack of sunlight, fruit trees and lush flowers grew. A stream fed the green lawn and little birds fluttered from one branch to the next. Four glass vases overflowing with golden coins sat on top of four earthen mounds.

At the end of the garden they found a flight of stairs that led even farther down into the earth. Since there was little light, the group clung to one another until they came to a set of double doors that seemed to be made from pure gold. Puck pushed them open to reveal a room overflowing with jewels and precious metals. Several torches illuminated the room and the light bounced off every sparking treasure, nearly blinding Sabrina. In the center of all the treasure she could make out two figures. The first was a short, balding man. The second was a toddler.

"So you found me," Mirror said. The youngest member of the Grimm family sat at his feet, burbling happily.

Daphne moved to rush to the boy, but Mirror's eyes ignited with magic and Sabrina pulled her back.

"And you've come to stop me?"

"Mirror, we could have found another way to get you what you want," Sabrina said.

Mirror shook his head. "I've waited long enough." He leaned down and snatched a golden lamp from a pile of treasure. It was nothing special compared to the treasures that surrounded it, but Mirror eyed it greedily. It was then that Sabrina realized they must be in the story of Aladdin—one of the many magical tales from *A Thousand and One Nights*. She knew what Mirror's lamp could do.

"Don't do this," she begged.

Mirror eyed the lamp. "It's my only chance. The place I need to go can't be reached any other way but by magic, and this little lamp, if it is anything like the real McCoy, has even more power than the Blue Fairy, Baba Yaga, and the Wicked Queen combined. This thing can change the future, the past—it could make me a god. Sadly, all that won't stick once I'm outside of this book and the Editor revises it away. What I need is in my story, which the Editor can't touch once I've changed it."

For a split second, Sabrina thought she saw remorse in the little man's face, but then he polished the lamp against his jacket. There was a strange energy in the air—a building of pressure that pressed against Sabrina's eardrums. A loud pounding rocked the cavern and then the energy formed itself into a single massive being standing nearly twenty feet tall. Its eyes were furious bonfires. Its skin was green and ghostly.

Its arms and chest were thick with stringy muscles, though its lower body remained mist-like and filled with crackling light. The creature looked down at them and snarled, "Who summons me?"

Mirror raised his hand. "That would be me."

"As my obligation, I must grant you three wishes, but I have been trapped in this lamp for eons. You would be most kind to use one of your wishes to grant me my freedom."

"You'll get no such satisfaction from me, genie," Mirror said.

The genie roared with rage and the temple's walls shook. Dust fell from the ceiling. Sabrina worried if it might cave in on her.

"Tantrums will not help," Mirror said, seemingly unfazed. "I released you from the lamp. I am your Master."

"You intend to change something," the creature seethed.

"Indeed, and before the Editor arrives with his creatures, I suggest we get to work. From what I understand, the magic in this book is as powerful as the magic of the real world. You possess the same power as your real-life counterpart?"

"I do, until I am revised," the genie snarled. "You have your wishes for a brief time, Master."

"I only need a moment. I wish the child and I were in the story of Snow White and the Seven Dwarfs," Mirror said.

"That story is off-limits," the genie said. "There are barriers to entrance."

"Did you not just say you are powerful? In the real world, a genie is beyond limits. It can raise the dead, change the course of rivers, and make the world bow at its master's feet. Use your powers to remove the barrier," Mirror commanded. "I want to go there. Do as I command."

The genie bent over and peered at him with angry eyes. "Very well." He clapped his hands. There was a mighty explosion and Mirror and the baby boy began to shimmer as if thousands of lightning bugs were crawling under their skin. Soon the light grew so bright that Sabrina could not look. She shielded her eyes until it faded. By then, Mirror and her brother were gone.

"Send us, too," Daphne said.

The genie shook his proud head. "I cannot. Mirror is my master. He has two more wishes for me to grant. I cannot offer you any help, even though I would truly like to destroy him."

"We have to get out of here," Daphne said. "We need to find a door."

Pinocchio shook his head. "We won't. The story hasn't ended. The door will never come."

Sabrina felt like she had been slapped. "You mean we're stuck here?"

Pinocchio nodded.

Sabrina leaned against a column and slid to the floor. They had failed. Mirror was changing history and getting whatever it was he set out to do. He would take her brother's body and use his magic to conquer the world. She remembered the terrible and bleak future she had seen when she and her sister had fallen into a time tear—humans were hunted by dragons and the world was on fire. She had hoped that she and her sister had made enough changes in the present to prevent that future. Now it looked as if it were all in vain.

And then a blast of wind blew her hair back and there were three figures standing over her.

"Why the long face, *liebling*?" Granny Relda said. Sabrina's mother, Veronica, and her father, Henry, were standing behind her.

Sabrina stood up and rushed into their arms. Daphne did the same. It wasn't long before all four of the Grimm women were in tears.

"We're going to have to have a very long talk, young ladies, about rushing headfirst into danger without your family," Henry scolded. "But first . . ."

He swept the girls into his arms and lifted them off the ground for a huge embrace. Though her father was tall and thin, almost wiry, she had forgotten how strong he could be. "Are you OK? Have you been hurt? Are you hungry?" There were a million questions.

"How did you find us?" Sabrina asked instead of answering.

"After Pinocchio opened all the doors in the Hall of Wonders, the monsters tore through the house. We were worried about your safety and came looking," Veronica said.

Granny nodded. "I'm afraid that much of our home is destroyed. All that we could salvage was the magic mirror, so we brought it out into the yard and started searching for you three inside the Hall of Wonders. Eventually we found the room with the Book of Everafter. We were examining it when the White Rabbit hopped out of the pages. Your father snatched him up and we took the magic yarn from him. I knew what it was instantly. We have the real one stored in the magical fabrics room—or at least we did. There was a lot of pillaging when the monsters were let out."

"I had to threaten to turn his feet into key chains, but he eventually told us how he had deserted you," Veronica said.

"He wasn't too happy that we tossed him right back into the Book," Granny said. "But the world does not need two White Rabbits."

"The world doesn't need one," Sabrina added.

"Then we used the yarn to bring us here. Wherever 'here' is."

"We're in the story of Aladdin, Mom," Henry said, waving toward the towering genie, who waited patiently. "My biggest question is," he said, "why did you jump into this book?"

"Mirror is the Master," Sabrina said. "We followed him in here."

Granny Relda nearly fainted. "That can't be possible. Our Mirror?"

"He's been behind all the troubles in Ferryport Landing. He has helped plot out all the bad stuff that has happened to us. Jack worked for him—Rumpelstiltskin, the Mad Hatter, Mrs. Heart, Nottingham, they are all part of the Scarlet Hand—the group he created!"

Granny Relda looked on the verge of tears.

"And he's not finished with us," Sabrina said. "He's got one more plan. It involves the baby."

Sabrina looked to her mother. Veronica had kept her secret as long as she could.

"Henry, I don't know how to tell you this," Veronica said as she took her husband's hand into her own. "The night we were abducted, I had an important announcement."

"The night we were poisoned and put to sleep?"

Veronica nodded. "I was going to tell you that we were going to have a baby."

Henry blinked. Then he blinked, again. "A baby?"

Veronica nodded.

"Veronica! We have to get you out of this book. This could be too dangerous. You need to be at home, resting, taking vitamins, other baby stuff like that."

Veronica shook her head. "This is going to be shocking."

And then Veronica told Henry about the baby boy that had been born during the two years they had been asleep. She told him about the magic that was used on her that helped Mirror deliver the child and that she herself didn't know the baby had been born until the night the Scarlet Hand had attacked the fort. She apologized to him for not telling him right away, but she saw he was under pressure, and to keep him safe she decided to wait until some of the chaos in the town subsided. She didn't need him running off into the night in search of the child.

"And that's why we're here," Daphne said. "Mirror had a nursery hidden in the Hall of Wonders. He's been taking care of Joshua ever since."

"Joshua?"

"I've been trying to come up with a name for him," Daphne said.

"I have a son . . . ," Henry said.

Veronica burst into happy tears, as did Granny Relda.

"You can name him whatever you want," Daphne said, sheepishly. "None of my ideas have really stuck."

"I was a big fan of Oohg," Puck said. "But personally, Puck is a wonderful name for a boy."

Henry raised an eyebrow.

Daphne's expression turned serious. "The point is that Mirror has the baby and he brought him into this book. He can use it to change history. If he does . . . something bad is going to happen."

"Bad in what way?" Granny asked.

Sabrina continued for Daphne. "He's going to try to steal our brother's body for himself. He wants to be real, not an Everafter—and not trapped in the Mirror. He'll have all his powers, and as a human child he can step through Wilhelm's magic barrier into the real world."

"And you helped?" Granny said as she turned her attention to Pinocchio. "Your father will not be happy when he hears about this."

Pinocchio scowled.

Granny Relda reached into her handbag and dug through a

dump truck's worth of makeup, pencils, binoculars, a pad of paper, and eventually a leather-bound book straight from the family's collection of journals.

"What's that?" Sabrina said.

"The journal of one Trixie Grimm," Granny said. "Your great-aunt. She was quite a character—an unrepentant bohemian who spent her time painting and marrying an endless stream of rich men. She walked down the aisle more than a dozen times and traveled the world before taking on the family business. She was a real can-do type. She negotiated a treaty between cyclopes and centaurs, helped Little Bo Peep find her sheep, and most importantly, had some experience inside the pages of the Book of Everafter."

Granny flipped through the pages. "She wrote extensively about the Book of Everafter and its origins, but most importantly she wrote about how magic linked the Book to actual history. She was integral in creating safety standards to make sure the stories remained unaltered. Even then she knew the Book was dangerous to have lying around so she locked it in a room in the Hall of Wonders. She didn't even label it. Most of the family didn't know it even existed."

"Mirror knew," Veronica said.

"Well, come along," Granny Relda said. "We have a baby boy to rescue."

The old woman whispered into the ball of yarn, "Lead us to the story of Snow White." It popped and crackled but sat still. "Something seems to be wrong."

"The Editor told us that story was off-limits," Daphne said.

"The Editor?" Henry said.

"Yes, the guardian of the Book," Granny said. "Trixie helped invent him. After the magic messed with the Book, she discovered that someone needed to put the stories back together if they were changed. He is described as the man in charge. I suppose we should pay him a visit. Come along, children."

"That's not going to be so easy," Daphne said. "The only way to get into his library is if he opens the door himself."

"And we kind of irked him," Puck said. "He's very sensitive."

"So I've heard. Trixie writes that she was startled by his bad attitude and suspected there would come a day when he would become difficult. I suppose that's why she placed this key inside," Granny Relda reached into her handbag and took out a bright golden key. "It won't get us into any of the other stories, but Trixie said it would get us into his library. Once we get there we're just going to have to use our considerable charms to convince him to let us follow Mirror into Snow White's tale."

Granny flipped through the Book, read a small passage to herself, and then stuffed the Book back into her handbag. Then she leaned over as if inserting the key into an actual lock. Suddenly, a door appeared in front of her around the key. She opened it and a blast of wind nearly knocked off her bonnet.

After the wind died down, they could hear the familiar sound of pages turning and a fireplace crackling. Granny reached out for the children and hurried everyone in ahead of herself.

"I wish you luck," Daphne said, turning to the genie.

The creature nodded respectfully as the family disappeared through the portal.

• • •

"Well, that was most disagreeable," Granny Relda said once they stepped into the Editor's study. She took her journal out of her handbag and jotted a note: "The doors between stories are best traveled with empty stomachs."

The Editor sat in his leather chair, a single reviser resting at his feet, licking its huge mouth as if it had just finished the last bite of a bucket of fried chicken. When he saw them, the Editor leaped from his chair as if shocked.

"How did you get in here?"

"Allow me to introduce myself," Granny said, ignoring his question. "My name is Relda Grimm."

"More Grimms? How many of them are there?" the man said dryly.

Granny ignored the sarcasm. "I believe you know my grandchildren, Sabrina and Daphne, as well as Puck. This is my son, Henry, and my daughter-in-law, Veronica. We are descendants of Trixie Grimm."

"A most troublesome woman, even if she did have a hand in my creation. She's very much responsible for many of my personal headaches—and that pesky streak appears to run in the family," the Editor said, flashing a dark look at the girls.

"Well, hopefully my request will be quick and painless," Granny replied. "We have need of your services."

The Editor's face fell in shock. "You come to me for help? You realize your granddaughters and this poor excuse for a Trickster King have caused me nearly a million times the grief of any Trixie? After making a deal with me, they raised an army of characters who attacked me in my own sanctuary. They attempted to aid them in their quest to escape the Book."

"Sabrina!" Henry said.

"That's not exactly what happened," Sabrina said sheepishly.

"We weren't helping them, Dad," Daphne added.

"Mr. Editor, I highly doubt my daughters are capable of betraying you," Veronica said.

"And I'm hardly a poor excuse for a Trickster King. I'm the first and the best, pal. Everyone after me is a copy," Puck said indignantly.

"Perhaps we can start over," Granny said. "I can assure you we will not be helping anyone escape this book. In fact, we're here to remove two individuals who have no business being in your pages. There's a man running through the stories carrying a child. We believe he has found his way into the tale known commonly as 'Snow White and the Seven Dwarfs.' We tried to chase him, but there seem to be barriers preventing our entrance. We'd like you to let us into the story. When we catch him, we'll all leave and you won't have any more problems from us."

"The magic mirror. I know all about him and the boy," the Editor said. "I have revisers chasing them as we speak."

"You can't!" Daphne cried. "They might hurt the baby."

"I have no concerns for the child," the Editor said. "My only goal is to keep these stories safe."

"Then you won't help us?" Henry said.

The Editor shook his head.

Henry rushed to the old man and snatched him by the collar.

He pushed him hard against a bookshelf and several volumes tumbled down on their heads. "That's my child in that story. If he gets hurt and you could have prevented it . . . well, there's nothing a skinny, magical entity with a lousy attitude could do to save himself."

The Editor eyed him closely. "I will not help."

Henry pulled back with a closed fist, but before he could punch the man, Granny stopped him.

"Let him go, Henry. I think we can persuade him without violence."

Henry shoved him once more but then released him. The Editor brushed off his suit and eyed the family. "Do you, now?"

"Yes, indeed," the old woman said as she stepped over to the magic door and whispered something into her ball of magic yarn. When she opened the door, the wind carried the smell of wheat into the room and howled over her voice. "If you think the children kept you busy, you have never had to experience me. Come along, family."

"What are we going to do?" Daphne said as she stepped into the void.

"Some good old-fashioned troublemaking," Granny Relda said with a grin, and then turned to Puck. "Why don't we show the Editor here why they call you the Trickster King?"

Puck smiled and leaped into the void.

"What about me?" Pinocchio cried.

"Stay here," Granny said with a smile. "I suspect we'll be right back."

She pushed the door open and her bonnet nearly flew off her head. Sabrina slipped her hand into her grandmother's and, along with the rest of her family, she stepped through the open doorway and vanished.

9

he stately study was replaced with a dusty road framed by wheat so dry and white one could almost hear its cries for rain.

"Where are we, Mom?" Henry said.

"Henry, I'm disappointed." The old woman smiled. "This is the setting for one of the most important fairy tales ever told. And if I'm correct, all the action is just over that rise."

Puck ran ahead while the family followed. When they reached the top of the crest, they looked down on a little valley. Three tiny structures rested along the road: one made from hay, the second from twigs, and the last from brick.

Daphne bit her palm and squeaked, "Pucktastic," but Sabrina's little sister's happiness was short-lived. A hulking, hairy creature lumbered in front of the grass house. It was the Big Bad Wolf and in his clawed hand he held a tiny whistle. When he used it, a magical wind as powerful as a tornado blasted the little house of straw, exploding it in every direction. When the house was gone, all that was left was a pig with a familiar face. The family's friend and former sheriff Ernest Hamstead was desperately grasping at a patch of turf, close to succumbing to the terrible wind. Before long, he lost his grip and was sent squealing and sailing across the valley.

"Not cool," Daphne said.

"And he's headed to the house of twigs now," Veronica said. "I never liked this story. It's depressing."

"I think it's hilarious," Puck said. "Really! I might wet myself if he does it again."

"There goes the house of twigs," Henry said. The wolf had unleashed his whistle on it with similar results. Mr. Swineheart had been hiding inside, but soon enough he was airborne as well, and disappearing into the clouds.

Puck was on his back, rolling around and giggling like a hyena. "Classic!"

"He's going to have some problems with the next house, Puck. Why don't you help him?"

"Relda!" Veronica cried.

"Really?" Puck said, wiping away happy tears.

"Go have fun," the old woman said.

Puck ran off to join the Big Bad Wolf.

"Relda, that's not nice," Veronica said.

"That's not our Mr. Boarman. He's just an approximation," Granny said. "The Editor will put this all back together the way it should be. If anything, we're just inconveniencing him."

Sabrina watched Puck encourage the Big Bad Wolf to huff and puff again, but he was unable to cause the well-built brick structure any harm. So Puck spun on his heels and his body inflated and two enormous ivory tusks grew out of his face. Soon he had become a prehistoric woolly mammoth. He dipped his head down and charged at the front door of the house, knocking it off its hinges. The Wolf hopped around happily, and he raced into the house with his tongue hanging out of his mouth. A second later Sabrina heard the growls and squeals of a horrible fight.

A door appeared before the group, and Puck rushed back to join them.

"I did good, old lady?" he said.

Granny nodded and mussed the boy's hair. "You did very good, Puck."

Out of the corner of her eye, Sabrina spotted revisers rushing down the street toward the brick house. As if on cue, Granny Relda kneeled down and spoke to the ball of yarn. "We want to go to Rapunzel."

She opened the door and everyone stomped through.

• • •

The group stood before a steep ivory tower. In a window near the top was a beautiful princess with the longest red hair Sabrina had ever seen. It hung down the side of the tower. The woman had braided it so that it was as thick and long as a rope. Climbing up the hair was a man, and on closer examination Sabrina realized it was Prince Charming.

Granny reached into her handbag and took out a pair of scissors. She handed them to Puck, who giggled with delight. A moment later, his wings were out and he was airborne. He fluttered above the prince, who was very high off the ground, and then started slicing the hair-rope in two. It wasn't long before Puck had cut completely through it. Prince Charming fell to the ground and landed with his leg in a very unnatural position.

Before long, the revisers were munching away on the story and Granny found another door. The old woman whispered to the yarn that she wanted to visit Cinderella.

When they passed through the doorway, the family found themselves on top of a grand staircase as a beautiful blond woman in a crystal blue dress raced past them and down the stairs. She stumbled a bit and fell, losing her shoe. Once again, Prince Charming appeared, chasing her down the stairs.

Cinderella was met at the foot of the stairs by a pumpkin-shaped coach, but before the driver could help her inside, Granny told Puck to steal it. The boy flew down the stairs, leaped into the driving seat, and shoved the footman to the ground. He grabbed the reins and sped off, leaving Cinderella stranded in front of Charming's castle. A moment later, a shimmering light engulfed the beautiful woman and she magically transformed back into a filthy, overworked housecleaner.

"Holy moly," Daphne said, squeezing her nose. "She's got the funk."

Prince Charming raced to her side with the glass slipper in his hands. "Excuse me, but are you the owner of—aw geez, what is that smell?"

Cinderella ran off into the night, sobbing into her hands.

"Pretty girl, but not a big fan of the soap, is she?" Prince Charming said to Henry.

A door appeared behind them as Puck returned. His clothes were covered with the insides of a pumpkin. "That buggy changed while I was on it," he complained. "I smell like a pie."

"You are doing very well," Granny said as revisers scurried up the staircase toward them. She whispered to the yarn and then opened the new door. "Let's see what we can mess with in Hansel and Gretel's story."

• • •

The family was soon standing before a life-size gingerbread house with candy-cane windowpanes, a roof made of peanut brittle, and a walkway lined with gumdrops.

"I don't think the children have showed up yet," Granny said. "Puck, are you feeling hungry?"

The boy clapped his hands and rubbed them together greedily. "Starving! I can't seem to get enough to eat these days."

"It's because you're becoming a teenager," the old woman explained.

Puck ignored her and sprang on the house, ripping parts of roof down and licking the door. He shoveled everything from the doorknob to the welcome mat into his mouth. In a matter of seconds, he was covered from head to toe in sticky, sugary candy. Cream filling was in his hair and icing ran down his shirt.

"Um, can I help with this one?" Daphne said.

Veronica laughed. "Be my guest."

Daphne dove in with the same enthusiasm as Puck. She licked the windows and took a giant bite out of the house's chewy foundation.

As she ate, two dumpy kids approached. They looked perplexed by the sight of other children already eating away at the house. Daphne spotted them and waved them off. "Just go home, kids.

A witch lives here. She'll put you in a cage and try to fatten you up. It's an ugly story. Besides, birds are eating your trail of bread crumbs, so you better hurry."

"Knuckleheads!" Puck said. "Didn't you think animals might want to eat the bread? Next time why don't you just leave a trail of winning lottery tickets?"

Hansel and Gretel looked offended and walked back the way they came.

"Here come the revisers," Sabrina said, nodding at the edge of the forest. Luckily a door appeared in clearing.

"All right," Granny said. "Let's see if the Editor likes what we do to the Frog Prince. I think we can get the princess to try some frog legs for dinner."

The family stepped through the void, but they did not land where they had aimed. Instead they found themselves back in the Editor's library. The Editor was staring at them with shock and exasperation. Pinocchio had settled in a corner and barely looked up from the giant book on his lap.

"Enough. Enough! ENOUGH!!!! The chaos is overwhelming. I can't keep up. You have to stop this assault on the Book right now."

"There's a very simple way to get us to stop," Granny Relda said. "Let us into Snow White's story."

The Editor scowled. "Don't you understand? It's off-limits for a reason! It is unstable."

"Don't *you* understand? I don't care," the old woman said. "My name is Relda Grimm. I am the wife of Basil Grimm. The mother of Henry and Jacob Grimm and mother-in-law of Veronica Grimm. I'm the grandmother of Sabrina and Daphne, and adopted grandma to Puck. I am also the grandmother of the little boy Mirror has kidnapped. Now that we have been properly introduced, you should know one more thing about me—I will do anything to protect my family. I don't care what falls apart. I don't care if the whole world falls apart."

"Mirror is already there," Sabrina said. "It will have to be revised anyway. What difference does it make now if we go there too?"

"All the difference in the world." The Editor's voice dropped to a murmur. "He is there too."

"He who?" Henry asked.

"I've told you of the great calamity that struck this book when a member of the Everafter community manipulated the magic that fuels it. I've also told you that a character was completely deleted—wiped from existence like he had never existed, not only in the Book but also in the real world. But what I have discovered since then is you can't completely delete anything. You can only hide it. So I put him in the margins of the story where he couldn't escape. He's hidden between the lines and he's still there and if you and Mirror and whoever walk in and start making big changes, you might tear history apart and let him out. And trust me—you do not want to let him out."

"We have to take the chance," Veronica said. "We won't stop until we find our boy."

If the Editor did not believe the family's commitment up to that point, he seemed to understand it now. His resolve collapsed, like a boxer who has finally run out of gas in the ring. He looked toward the ceiling.

"Might I have your attention?" he called. A moment later, hundreds, if not thousands, of fat, hungry revisers climbed down the walls. They gathered at his feet, turning their blank faces up to him.

"There is a man invading Snow White's tale," he said, which caused the little creatures to erupt into nervous chatter. "He may cause a great deal of problems for the real world. I wish to remove him from our book and to do whatever we need to do to undo some of the barriers that prevent others from entering."

The creatures let out some excited twittering that sent a chill up Sabrina's back.

"No, you cannot revise him. You won't recognize him because

he is walking through events he experienced himself. Normally, I would send you to completely revise the tale, but there is another visitor from the real world—a small child—an innocent. This child must not be revised."

There were more squeaks. These seemed to Sabrina like arguments.

"No, the child must be spared. You are *not* to revise him. We are attempting to rescue him."

There was more chatter, and the Editor frowned. He turned to the family.

"They understand, but whether they will obey me is another story. They have their roles as I have mine. The best I can do is give you a head start."

"What about me?" Pinocchio called. "You're not sending me back into that book, are you?"

The Editor shot him an angry look. "You're staying here. I think you've caused enough trouble, little boy."

The thin man stepped over to a door that materialized by the fireplace. He opened it and gestured into the emptiness beyond. The family rushed through.

"Find him," the Editor begged. "Find Mirror and the boy and leave my book as quickly as you can."

• • •

When the raging wind in their ears died away and the flickering lights stopped blinding Sabrina, she looked around. She and her family were standing in the middle of a crude cabin. A group of seven very short men were standing around watching a beautiful woman sweep the rough, wooden floor.

"Well, who's hungry?" the woman said, setting down her broom. She turned and flashed everyone a smile as bright as a spotlight. She was a collection of perfect features—a delicate button nose, bright red lips, skin like cream, hair as black as night, and bright blue eyes that sparkled like jewels.

"Ms. White!" Sabrina said.

Snow White looked confused. "Have we met?"

"She's not our Ms. White," Granny Relda said. "She's just walking history."

Sabrina eyed the beautiful woman closely. Since stepping into the Book of Everafter, they had met many fairy-tale versions of people they knew in the real world, but most had been nothing more than acquaintances (or, in the case of the Queen of Hearts, bitter enemies). Snow White was a very good friend of her family. Sabrina had spoken to her hundreds of times, and now, with this copy right before her eyes, her brain was having a difficult time separating the two.

"Snow, you can't let anyone into this house," one of the little men said, completely butting into the conversation. Sabrina turned and realized the speaker was another good friend, Mr. Seven. He was carrying a mug of something that turned his face red every time he took a sip.

"Your mother is trying to kill you," another dwarf said.

"I know, I know," Snow said as if it were nothing to worry about.

"She's already disguised herself as a peddler and choked you with a strand of lace," a bearded dwarf complained.

"Then you stuck that poisoned comb in your hair. Luckily we came home from the mine before it killed you," a bald dwarf added.

"You need to be on guard and not let anyone in when we are not with you," Mr. Seven said.

Snow White smiled as if she was thinking of something else and went back to sweeping the floor. "I'll do my best. I guess I'm just so gullible."

"Well, we better get back to work," Mr. Seven said as he took a long, deep drink. His breath smelled like fruit and alcohol. "Keep the doors locked."

"Will do!" Snow said, but it was clear she wasn't listening.

The dwarfs shuffled out of the house, leaving the family alone with the beauty. She turned to face them, confused.

"Still here?"

"You haven't noticed a magic mirror running around here with a little boy, have you?" Henry asked.

Snow White set her broom down. Her expression shifted from ditzy to deadly serious. "Have you come to change history again? These events have been revised already." She rushed to the window and peered out as if concerned that she might be overheard. "The Editor worked on it himself. Is he unhappy with how it's going?"

Suddenly, there was a rap at the door.

"That's the Wicked Queen," Snow said. "You should hide. We shouldn't alter anything more. It was hard getting it to make sense after all the changes."

Everyone argued, but eventually Snow convinced them all to hide under beds and listen as the story unfolded. Once everyone was out of sight, Snow went to an open window.

"I am not allowed to let anyone in. The dwarfs have forbidden me to do so."

An old woman's voice croaked from the other side of the window. "That is all right with me. I'll easily get rid of my apples. Here, I'll give you one of them."

"Don't do it," Daphne whispered.

"Hey, marshmallow, your knee is in my back," Puck groaned.

"Hush!" Sabrina ordered, and then turned back to Snow and the witch.

"No, I can't accept anything," Snow replied to her visitor.

"Are you afraid of poison? Look, I'll cut the apple in two. You can eat the red half, and I shall eat the white half."

Sabrina heard someone take a bite from the apple. A moment later, Snow White collapsed onto the floor. Sabrina watched the old woman stand over her.

"White as snow, red as blood, black as ebony wood. This time the dwarfs cannot awaken you."

When the old woman was gone, the family climbed out from under the bed and hovered over Snow White.

"The people in these stories are nuts," Sabrina said. "She knew the witch was coming, but she went through with the whole thing anyway."

Puck shook Snow. "Wakey-wakey, sleepyhead."

"She's enchanted," Sabrina explained. "She won't wake up until someone who truly loves her kisses her on the lips."

"So this fairy tale is a horror story," Puck said.

"The prince will be along to wake her up soon," Granny said as Veronica helped her out from beneath the bed. "We should get back to looking for Mirror and the baby. Whatever he plans on doing to your son is going to happen soon."

In the silence after Granny finished speaking, Sabrina heard the unmistakable sound of someone taking another crunchy bite of the apple. She turned to find Puck with a mouthful of fruit. "Can't we stop and get something to eat? This puberty thing is making me all kinds of hungry. Oh!" He looked down at the apple sheepishly and then fell to the floor in a heap.

"No way," Henry said.

"I can't believe you!!!" Sabrina shouted at the unconscious boy. If he had been awake she might have kicked him. "Where is your brain?"

"In his defense, I don't think he knows this story," Daphne said. "His parents probably didn't read him too many fairy tales when he was little . . . four thousand years ago."

"Aaargh!" Sabrina growled. "We have to find Mirror and stop him—not carry Sleepy Steven around. What do you think we should do?"

"We'll put Puck into one of these beds," Henry suggested. "He'll be safe here. When it's all said and done, we'll come back and get him."

"What about the revisers?" Sabrina said as her father hauled Puck's limp body to the nearest cot. "What if they come before we get back?"

"We'll watch him," the dwarfs said as they entered the room.

Mr. Seven was in the lead. "The Editor filled us in. Hopefully you can stop the magic mirror from unleashing that madman. Follow the path to the castle. That's where you'll find Mirror."

"What madman?" Veronica asked.

"It's not important," Mr. Three said. "Just go!"

Sabrina nodded, glancing once more at the boy fairy. She had never seen him look so vulnerable. She had gotten used to his bravado, and she realized his confidence gave her a sense of assurance that everything would be OK in the end. Now she had to admit she preferred his sneering and jokes to his silence and helplessness.

"C'mon, *lieblings*," Granny Relda said as she pushed the cottage door open.

"There it is," Daphne said, pointing up the road to a castle sitting high on a hill. It was enormous and built from black stones. Its two towers bore black flags that fluttered in the wind.

"Great," Sabrina grumbled. "Nothing like a spooky castle for an ultimate showdown."

They ran up the hill to the imposing castle. With their legs aching and their lungs tight, they raced across the castle's drawbridge. Below them the waters were filled with horrible leathery crocodiles and spiked beasts. Sabrina shook off a chill and ran through the open doors of the castle. The main room was filled with paintings of an elegant woman with dark hair dressed in royal robes. In one depiction, her hand rested on the head of a cheetah. Sabrina recognized her at once; she was Bunny Lancaster—also known as the Wicked Queen—also known as Snow White's mother. But there was no sign of Mirror or any other characters in the room.

Sabrina took a deep breath and helped her grandmother scale the stairs at the back of the entrance hall. When they reached the top, they huffed and puffed their way down a long, empty hallway, only to face another completely different flight of stairs.

"Can't anyone do their evil on the first floor?" Henry complained.

"Or at least put in an elevator," Daphne said.

They climbed the second flight and were stopped in their tracks by a heavy wooden door. Through it the girls heard a terrified scream followed by a jarring crash of broken glass.

"Stay close," Henry whispered to the family, and he pushed the door. When it swung open, the family witnessed a horrible scene. Mirror had his hands wrapped around the slender throat of the Wicked Queen. Despite his tiny frame, the man had hoisted her off the floor. Her face was turning blue and her feet were kicking wildly in vain for the solid ground.

"Hello, everyone," Mirror said without tearing his attention away from the Queen. "If you would just give me a moment here with my mother, I will soon give you my undivided attention."

Mirror tossed the woman into a corner. She stared at him apprehensively as she struggled to breathe. "You look bewildered, Mommy. Are you surprised your son is angry? Of all the people in the world, you should know why! You locked me inside that prison! Then you gave me away!"

His shouts, full of a terrifying rage, echoed off the walls and rang in Sabrina's ears. She was well aware of Mirror's magical abilities, but at that moment it was his tone that scared her the most. It seemed to have an effect on the others, too. In the far corner of the room a small child let out a whimpering cry. It was her baby brother!

Henry spotted him too, and raced to him, but a blast of lightning from Mirror's hands stopped him in his tracks.

"Not so fast, Hank," Mirror said.

"You have to stop this," the Wicked Queen choked. "You're messing with very fragile history."

"I've been abused and mistreated for centuries," Mirror continued, ignoring her pleas. "Then you turned your back on me as if I were property. What kind of mother are you?"

"I am not your mother," the Wicked Queen said. "If you've come for revenge, you should have stayed in the real world."

Mirror's eyes glowed and the air crackled. He stuck out an angry finger at the woman. "As always, you deny me."

The reflection in a full-length mirror leaning against the wall swirled and bubbled. The frame was familiar to Sabrina. It was identical to the one they had in Granny Relda's home. Soon, a bulbous and intimidating face appeared. It was the storybook version of Mirror himself, and his expression was panicked.

"You must stop this," the man in the mirror said. "The story will collapse."

Mirror approached the enchanted glass. "So, this is what I look like on the other side? I'm really quite impressive."

"There is no need for this violence," the fake magic mirror said.

Mirror thrust his hand into the reflection. He wrapped his fingers around his doppelgänger's throat and squeezed.

"What do you want?" the Wicked Queen said as she climbed to her feet.

After a long and painful moment, Mirror released him and stalked back to the Wicked Queen. "I want you to use your considerable magical talents to make me real. I want—"

Suddenly, there was a tremendous rocking sensation. Everything was shaking—the ground, the air, even the colors of objects scattered around the room. Sabrina felt like she was inside a snow globe in the hands of a hyperactive child.

"What was that?" Mirror said.

"I told you this story is unstable," the Queen said. "It can't take any more revision. It's all going to fall apart."

"Then we better get crackin'," Mirror said, pulling the Queen across the room.

"I can't make you real," the Queen stammered.

"Tsk tsk," he said. "You are the Wicked Queen, or at least a version of her. You possess her magic and her knowledge. If the real Queen knew how to create me, then so do you. This task should be effortless."

While they were arguing, Henry ran forward again. This time Mirror hit him with a blast of electricity and he flew across the room, crumpling to the ground against a stone wall. Veronica and Daphne rushed to his side.

"Bunny, we're all waiting," Mirror said.

The Wicked Queen looked around as if hoping a hero on a white horse might charge through the door and save her, but then her shoulders slumped in surrender. She crossed the room to where a dozen empty frames leaned against a table covered in a tarp. She removed the covering to reveal several jars filled with slithering blobs of black glop. Whatever it was, it seemed to be alive. "You don't understand, Mirror. When I create a magical looking glass, I'm not creating a life. You are an enchantment, a spell—nothing more than a few rare ingredients and an ancient incantation. Once you appeared, I placed you into an empty vessel and then shaped you into whatever form I needed. I'll show you."

The Wicked Queen opened one of the jars and removed the black glob. It slithered around her arm like a snake but she wrangled it back into her palms. At once her hand turned a bright, hot red and the creature shimmied and twisted like melting glass.

She spoke a few unintelligible words and one of the empty picture frames began to brighten like a television screen. Once it was bright white, she introduced the blob onto its surface. It sank in like she had dropped it into a bathtub. Then she placed her hand over the reflection. She uttered a few more words in an ancient language and then removed her hand. A scarlet handprint remained on the surface.

Mirror smiled. "That red handprint was the first thing I saw when I was born. I've seen it in my dreams ever since. It's quite a unique symbol—intimidating, powerful. Don't you agree, Relda? You must have seen it popping up all over Ferryport Landing."

Granny shook her head in disgust.

The red print faded and a face appeared in the frame. It was that of a burly man with short gray hair, a full beard, and a sweater. "Awaiting your instructions," it said in a gruff, almost salty tone.

Mirror gestured to the jars. "If you can put that energy into something you can take it out, correct?" Mirror said. "You could take it out of my body?"

The Queen's eyes grew wide. "I suppose I could, but I would need a vessel to place it into. I don't see the point of just putting you back into a mirror."

"Oh, no, I've done the mirror thing. Allow me to introduce my vessel," Mirror said. He snatched the baby Grimm off the floor and held him in his arms. "I want you to put me into him. He will give me my freedom not only from the magical cage you trapped me in, but also from the town of Ferryport Landing. I will be both Everafter and human at the same time."

"You want to possess him?" Mirror's storybook double cried.

Mirror nodded. "He is still a child. Whatever soul he has cannot be strong, so he will not fight me. Can you do it?"

The Wicked Queen nodded. "Yes, but—"

"No!" Veronica cried. "If you want a body, you can take mine!"

Mirror shook his head. "No offense, Veronica, but I'd like to live a long, full life. I want the boy."

Granny Relda growled. Sabrina had never seen her so angry. "None of this had to happen, Mirror. You could have come to me. I would have done everything in my power to set you free."

"Relda, that is kind of you to say. But you would have failed. One day you would have died and I would have had to start all over with a new owner. Your family has shown me great kindness, but who knows where I might have landed? I could be in the hands of tyrants someday. No, the time is now. I can't wait another day." He turned back to the Wicked Queen. "All right, Mom. It's time you finally gave me a birthday present."

The Wicked Queen stepped forward and her hand grew red once more.

"You may want to set the boy on the ground," she said. Mirror did as he was told and she placed her hand on Mirror's head. He screamed in agony as the hand burned his skin, and then a black glob, just like the ones in the jars, seeped out of his mouth and hovered before the man's blank eyes. When the Queen let go of him, Mirror's body collapsed to the ground, dead and empty. A moment later, it liquefied into a silver, reflective fluid, like mercury.

"Bunny, you don't have to finish this," Granny said.

The Queen shook her head. "If I don't, he'll take someone else in this room. Maybe even me. You don't want him to have my power."

She stood the boy up, waved her red hand just over his face, and the black blob shot into his mouth. If it hurt or distressed him, the baby showed no sign. The only change was the expression on his face. His youthful smile and glittering eyes were replaced with an ageless intelligence. The boy looked down at the silver puddle and studied his face in its reflection.

"Fascinating," he said. The single word told Sabrina that Mirror's plan had succeeded.

"No!" Veronica cried, bursting into tears. Henry's head fell in exhaustion.

The little boy turned to the Grimms. He lifted his little hands and his fingertips crackled with magical power. "Very good. My abilities work just as well."

"The Editor will fix this," Sabrina said. "He'll change you back to what you were."

"Oh, I'm afraid he's going to have his hands full with other problems," the boy said. "You see, while I was traveling through these books I learned that the Snow White history has been completely rebuilt from the ground up. Apparently, it was much different once—I don't recall what actually happened because someone changed it in this book and it wiped my memory. A troubling phenomenon, but one I intend to exploit. There's someone or something that is caged up in the margins. I can feel it. And if I can have my freedom, I suppose I can give it to someone else, too."

"How are you going to do that, Mirror?" Granny Relda said.

"By killing a main character," the child replied, his eyes glowing with power. His little body lifted off the ground and he flew through the castle window out into the sky. Sabrina and Daphne rushed to the window and saw him soaring like an eagle down toward the Seven Dwarfs' cottage.

Suddenly a door materialized and the Editor appeared in the doorway. His face looked panicked. "He's after Snow White! Queen, if he manages to kill someone that important, he will surely rip everything apart. We all have to stop him at any cost. You must help the Grimms!"

10

 ome with me," the Wicked Queen said, then hurried everyone down the many flights of stairs and into a stable where several saddled horses waited. Henry and Veronica helped the children and Granny Relda onto their mounts. They took two for themselves while the Wicked Queen mounted a frightening black stallion with angry eyes. Seconds later they were bolting down the path at a heart-racing speed.

"Revisers!" Daphne screamed, pointing to the side of the path. Hundreds of creatures were eating the trees and shrubs.

"Pray they work quickly," the witch said.

"Pray? Those things are monsters," Sabrina said.

"Those things may be the only way of keeping the story intact. If the bindings and rewrites the Editor established fall apart, then something far worse than a reviser will be let loose."

"Could you fill us in on what everyone's talking about? What's so important about this story?" Sabrina asked.

The Wicked Queen turned to the girls. "There was a time when Snow White's tale was much different—much more tragic."

When they got to the cottage, they found the dwarfs battling with Mirror, who zipped around in the air like a mosquito. Mr. Seven broke from the fight and rushed out to help the family off their horses. When she was on her feet, Sabrina saw two glass coffins resting on a platform in the garden. The lovely Snow White was resting in one. In the other was Puck. Despite all the excitement around them, neither of the slumbering people woke up.

"We spotted revisers over the hill," the Queen said.

"We've got a bigger problem. Prince Atticus is coming," Mr. Seven said.

"Who is Atticus?" Daphne asked.

A man on a great gray horse galloped out of the woods. Moments later, he leaped to his feet and sprang into action, joining the fight to stop Mirror.

"Atticus is my brother," he said, swinging his sword with all his might. Even with the odd, fake-looking colors of this world, Sabrina immediately recognized the Book's version of Ferryport Landing's former mayor, William Charming.

"Your brother?" Granny Relda said. "You don't have a brother!"

Charming ignored her. "The Editor came to me. He told me to fight. The real people must leave the Book at once. A door to the real world will appear at any moment."

"No, we won't go without the boy," Granny Relda said. She turned to Bunny Lancaster. "Can you remove Mirror from him?"

"Yes, but like I said, he'll just jump into one of us."

"Do it!" Granny begged.

The Queen's hand turned red once more. She waved it at the boy and his body flew toward her against his will. The burning hand clamped down on his head and Mirror's voice cried out for mercy. Then the little boy collapsed to the ground. Veronica raced to his side and swept him up into her arms. He began to cry from surprise and shock.

The Queen couldn't hold on to the black blob and it darted around the crowd, searching for a new vessel. It looked like a shapeless dog sniffing for a buried bone. As Sabrina watched, fascinated, it attacked, clamping down on her shoulders and trying to force its way into her mouth. She fought back, grinding her teeth to keep it from entering her, but the creature was strong. After a few moments of fighting, seemingly frustrated, it darted to her sister.

"Don't open your mouth!" Sabrina shouted. Daphne was doing all she could to fight it.

"I'm afraid we can't stop it," the Queen said. "It must find a body to possess."

A clarity came over Sabrina that she had never experienced before. She realized that when things were at their worst she could always find an answer. Sure, she had made many mistakes, but most of them were misjudgments fueled by prejudices, mistrust, or stubbornness. But when it was a matter of life and death involving a friend or loved one, she never made mistakes. When it came to protecting her family, the answers were always clear.

She raced to Daphne's side, but Granny Relda was already there. Sabrina knew what she was going to do. It was exactly what she had planned herself.

"Mom! *No!*" Henry shouted as he wrestled with a reviser.

Granny Relda turned and looked to her family. "He'll get out, Henry. We know he will. And he'll take some poor child or another Everafter who's already ripe with power. If he must possess someone, it should be a person nearing their final days;

someone old, and tired, with creaky joints and arthritis, and no magical ability. If he's going to take over the world, then the world should only have to suffer for so long."

"Granny!" Sabrina cried.

"I love you, *liebling*," Granny said, blowing kisses. "Take care of Puck—he's one of mine too."

She turned to the ghostly spirit attacking Daphne and buried her fingers into the blackness. "Let her go, Mirror!" Granny cried.

The creature resisted but she would not let go. Eventually, it surrendered and entered the old woman. Granny's face lost its rosy color. Her bright green eyes flashed white hot, and her sweet, soft smile disappeared. It was replaced with an angry scowl.

"You have ruined everything!" Mirror's voice bellowed out of the old woman. "Look at this body!"

"Vile creature," Prince Charming said. He waved his sword threateningly at Granny Relda. "Release your hold on that woman."

Mirror raised the old woman's wrinkled hand and sparks crackled from the tips of her fingers. "You ridiculous oaf. Do you think I would stay in this body if I had a choice?" Electricity charged out of Granny's hands and encircled the Prince's sword.

It yanked the weapon out of Charming's grasp and Granny took it. "My opportunity—stolen! So I will bring this world down around your ears."

Granny thrust the sword into Charming's gut. The Prince was stunned. Then he fell over and moved no more.

No sooner had he fallen than the world shook so violently that Sabrina was knocked backward to the ground. Her head slammed against the soil and her sneakers were blasted off her feet. Before she could stand and retrieve her shoes, there was a second explosion. This one was louder, and the blast of wind that accompanied it was so hot it scorched her face, neck, and hands. But the third explosion was the one that frightened her. It split columns in two and churned the ground like a pot of boiling water. Fissures formed, allowing skin-searing steam to escape from deep below. Along with it came an unearthly concoction of lights and sounds and colors. It wasn't a mist or a fog—it was alive, made from something old and angry. It spun into a whirlwind and surrounded the children.

"Everyone must go," the Wicked Queen shouted. "Atticus is coming!"

"Sabrina, this is not good!" Daphne shouted over the din. It was clear the little girl knew what was happening as well. "We have to stop it."

"Be my guest!" she cried. "If you haven't noticed, I don't have any magical powers. I'm not an Everafter. I'm just a girl from New York City."

And then there was a fourth and final explosion. A strange, red-haired man appeared over her. He wore a black tunic, heavy boots, and a long scabbard. In one hand he had what Sabrina would later find out was called a flail—a handle connected to a chain connected to a heavy steel ball. He looked at her and smiled, but it was not friendly. It was like a hungry tiger looking at his wounded prey. Then he glanced over at Prince Charming's lifeless body and he laughed.

"William, I'm disappointed," Atticus said. "I wanted to kill you myself."

In the confusion, Sabrina watched Granny Relda rush to the door that had materialized. She turned and looked back at the family. For a moment, her familiar eyes locked onto Sabrina, but then the old woman shook her head as if dizzy and her smile turned to a sneer. She darted through the doorway and disappeared.

"What is this?" Atticus said. "A doorway to the real world?"

No one answered. The man seemed to steal their confidence. Sabrina knew that she—or someone—should block his path. There was something in Atticus's face that made it clear the world was not ready for him, but her courage had vanished with Granny Relda.

A moment later, Atticus stepped through the portal and was gone as well.

"Kids, we have to go," Henry shouted as he scooped Puck's unconscious body out of its glass case. "The revisers are coming!"

Veronica clung to her baby boy and dashed through the doorway just as the pink creatures scuttled down the hillside. There were thousands of them, eating and ripping at the ground, the trees, even the air, leaving only a blank white plainness behind them.

"Grimms, you must leave," the Editor cried from the open doorway. "I cannot stop the revisers. This story is a page-one rewrite."

Daphne and Henry dashed forward into the abyss with Puck flung over Henry's shoulder. Sabrina looked out on the disappearing world, then followed.

• • •

After retrieving Pinocchio from the Editor's library and saying their strained good-byes to the Editor himself, the family locked the nameless door to the room that held the Book of Everafter and made the long trek out of the Hall of Wonders. Luckily, there was no sign of Atticus or their own possessed grandmother.

When they stepped through the portal into Granny's front yard, Sabrina stared, shocked and horrified. Very little of their home was left standing. When Pinocchio's marionettes had unlocked the doors of the Hall of Wonders, they had released all manner of terrible creatures. Those creatures had stampeded through the mirror and demolished what four generations of Grimms had called their own. Elvis, the family's two-hundred-pound Great Dane, raced forward. He knocked Daphne down and showered her with happy licks. She kissed him back and scratched behind his ears. Then she introduced the dog to the newest member of the family, though Veronica looked as if she would never let him go.

Henry set Puck on the ground and leaned against Granny's ancient car, which had surprisingly remained untouched in all the chaos, and then he went into the house. Despite Veronica's warnings that it was unsafe, he said he had to go back in to retrieve as many of the family journals as he could. When he returned, carrying a sack over his shoulder, he happily reported that he had saved all of them. He opened the trunk of the car and eased them inside. Then he set the magic mirror on top and closed the trunk carefully.

Pinocchio sat down in the yard as if unsure of what to do next. They all waited for a minute, silent.

"Well?" Daphne said to Sabrina.

"Well, what?"

"Are you going to wake Puck up?"

"We tried," Sabrina said. "He ate part of a poisoned apple."

"Did you kiss him?"

Sabrina wasn't sure she heard her sister correctly. "What?"

"You have to kiss him. He needs the kiss of someone who loves him."

"Absolutely not!" Henry shouted.

"It has to be a romantic kiss too," Daphne added slyly. "Listen, he's asleep, and if anyone knows about that spell it's the Grimm family. If there is even the teensiest chance that you love Puck, you have to kiss him."

"There's no chance at all!" Sabrina said, wracking her brain for a really great excuse. "I don't love him. It won't work."

"Then he'll sleep forever," Daphne said.

Sabrina looked at Puck. He was smelly, rude, mean, selfish, stupid, and immature. He wasn't the kind of boy that girls fell in love with. He was the kind of boy you stayed fifty yards from at all times. Kissing him wouldn't wake him up, but if everyone was going to pressure her, what else could she do? She'd kiss him and mentally remind herself to brush, floss, and gargle the first chance she got. She looked to her father, who seemed physically ill, while her mother smiled reassuringly. Daphne rolled her eyes. "Geez, enough with the buildup. Just do it."

Sabrina leaned in and pressed her lips to Puck's. There was a little static shock that startled her and she stepped back with her hands on her mouth.

"Oh!" It hadn't hurt. It was just . . . surprising.

Puck's eyes flickered open and he looked around. "So, what did I miss?"

• • •

The family spent the rest of the day retrieving what little was left intact in the house. Even Pinocchio helped, albeit reluctantly. Most of the time he groused about "child labor laws" and "indentured servitude." It gave Sabrina and Puck time to be alone. They sat in the yard and looked over the house for a while in silence.

Finally, Puck spoke. "Let's not change."

"Huh?"

"The insults. The pranks. Let's not change."

"I don't know what you're talking about."

"Someday you and I are getting married." Puck sighed, as if terribly depressed. "The cruel hand of fate will not allow us to escape it. Worse, my own body is betraying me. I'm getting older every day. So, in essence, we are up the river without a paddle. If we have to get married and have a million babies, I hope our relationship will be built on mutual disgust and an endless barrage of ridicule and insults. It feels like the only thing I can count on right now. I don't want something dumb like respect and affection getting in the way."

Sabrina laughed. "OK, on the outside chance that you and I do get married, I promise to insult you all day long. But you do realize there's a very good chance that you and I won't get married."

"That's not what you told me. You said you went to the future and we were married," Puck said. "We can't escape fate."

"We didn't see *the* future. We saw *a* future," Sabrina said. "The world we saw was terrible. The Master was in control of everything. Dragons hunted people. Human beings were refugees. When we got back to our time, Daphne and I started doing everything we could to prevent that from happening. And we have managed to change some stuff. For instance, Snow White was dead in the future but we saved her life. Daphne had a horrible scar on her face but we fixed that, too. There have been countless other things we stopped from happening. We may have altered the future so much that you and I don't get married."

Puck sat back, deep in thought. "So, you and I might not get married and have to do all that mushy stuff and have kids and buy a house and get a mortgage? I might not have to get a job or take baths or take up reading?"

Sabrina shook her head. "If we rescue Granny Relda and stop Mirror for good, we could probably change it all."

"Great! Let's kick Mirror's butt," he said.

Sabrina smiled at the joke but down deep it hurt her a little. Not that she wanted her whole life planned out for her when she was only twelve years old. She wanted there to be mysteries about the life she might lead and the loves she might find along the way, and she didn't want fate telling her whom she was supposed to be with. Still, Puck was special to her. He was her first kiss; her first crush. There was no use denying it anymore. Poisoned apples had spilled the beans.

"Thank you, Sabrina Grimm."

"For what?"

"Don't torture me! I won't say it out loud. Just . . . you know, in four thousand years no one has felt . . . Oh, just forget it!" he said. He took a strong whiff of the air. "Geez, Grimm. You're rank."

Then he walked away. A moment later, Daphne approached.

"Bobby is so cute," Daphne said.

"Bobby? You want to name the baby Bobby Grimm?" Sabrina said.

Before she could argue, their parents approached with the little boy in their arms.

"We've come up with a name," Veronica said.

"Please tell me it isn't Oohg," Sabrina replied.

"No, it's Basil, after my father." Henry beamed.

"I think it works," Daphne said.

"So, what's next?" Puck said, flying back to the group. "The old lady sacrificed herself, which means no more free meals for me. We have to get her back."

Henry sighed. "I'm not sure what to do first."

Sabrina looked around at her family. All of them were at a loss. They needed someone to step forward and lead them. For the first time in many days the thought did not make her ill.

"We need to start preparing," Sabrina said. "Mirror has some horrible plans. Worse still, that man he unleashed, Atticus—I saw his face, and he's not right. There isn't an ounce of humanity inside him. Puck, you find Uncle Jake, Mr. Canis, Charming, and Snow White. Take Pinocchio with you. Mom, Dad, Daphne—we need to go see the real Wicked Queen, and unfortunately, we're going to have to get some help from someone I'd rather not see again."

"Baba Yaga," Daphne groaned.

Sabrina nodded. "If we're going to stop Mirror, we're going to need this town's most powerful people. Because if we can't stop him, it may very well be the end of the world."

To be concluded . . .

ABOUT THE AUTHOR

Michael Buckley is the *New York Times* bestselling author of the *Sisters Grimm* and *NERDS* series. He has also written and developed television shows for many networks. Michael lives in Brooklyn, New York, with his wife, Alison, and his son, Finn.

This book was designed by Melissa Arnst, and art directed by Chad W. Beckerman. It is set in Adobe Garamond, a typeface that is based on those created in the sixteenth century by Claude Garamond. Garamond modeled his typefaces on those created by Venetian printers at the end of the fifteenth century. The modern version used in this book was designed by Robert Slimbach, who studied Garamond's historic typefaces at the Plantin-Moretus Museum in Antwerp, Belgium.

The capital letters at the beginning of each chapter are set in Daylilies, designed by Judith Sutcliffe. She created the typeface by decorating Goudy Old Style capitals with lilies.

HOW WILL IT END?

- Will Baba Yaga help the Grimms in their hour of need?
- What's the next step in the Master's dark plan, and can the Grimms stop him in time?
- Will Puck and Sabrina stop fighting long enough to admit . . . well, something?
- Will Jacob avenge Briar Rose's death?
- Can Sabrina and Daphne learn to trust each other again?
- Is love finally in the air for Snow and Charming?
- Will Sabrina finally be able to eat something normal without Granny in the kitchen?
- What is that disgusting smell? Elvis? Puck?
- How much wood would a woodchuck chuck if a woodchuck could chuck wood?

Don't miss the exciting conclusion of

THE *SISTERS GRIMM* SERIES

in Book Nine!
Visit www.sistersgrimm.com for updates.